GAY CITY 5

First Edition

GAY CITY HEALTH PROJECT
517 E. Pike Street
Seattle, WA 98122
www.GayCity.org

Many of these selections are works of fiction. Names, characters, places and incidents depicted are either
products of the contributors' imaginations or are used fictitiously. Any resemblance to actual persons,
living or dead, events or locales is entirely coincidental.

ISBN-13: 978-1489580146

ISBN-10: 148958014X

Volume edited by Evan J. Peterson

Cover design by John Coulthart

Book design by Anne Bean

Series created by Vincent Kovar

Printed in the United States of America

GAY CITY 5

Edited by Evan J. Peterson
Series Edited by Vincent Kovar

A Minor Arcana Press Incantation

Supporters

This volume of Gay City Anthologies is made possible thorough the support of...

Patron

Daniel Nye

Supporters

  Jonathan L. Bowman, Attorney at Law, P.S., proud Supporter of the Gay City Anthologies project from its inception, is pleased to continue his support of Gay City's vision by sponsoring *Ghosts in Gaslight, Monsters in Steam*.

Cantor David Serkin-Poole, Temple B'nai Torah, Bellevue, WA is proud to support the noble work of Gay City Health Project.

Kickstarter Backers

Jill Braden, Writer http://jillbradenwriter.blogspot.com/

Jennifer Gallison

Laura Treadway

Lisa J. Black

Callum James

Kerry Stanhope

Peter Jabin

Megan Clements

Matt Taylor

Studio Foglio

Jack Johnston

Dawn Oshima

Crystal Mechler

Lane Rasberry

Jennifer Lavoie

Richard May

Ulises Mark Chavez

tyrone bachus

Christian DeLay

Natasha Yar-Routh

verybookish

Chris MacGibbon

The Gay Cliché by Kevin Richards

Scott Glancy

To everyone who has dreamed along with me.
—Vincent

To the growing Minor Arcana Press tribe, and especially
to Anne Bean and Mykol Radziszewski, who help me lead.
—Evan

Act I: Victorian Venom

Act 2: Modern Monsters

"Why Do You Like That?"

Evan J. Peterson

My mother says the damnedest things without a speck of cruelty. She speaks her mind in a way that shows her to be incredibly genuine, innocently so:

"You've lost weight. Did the doctor check you for AIDS?"

"Do you think Jesus was from another planet?"

"Why do people buy their babies all these toys? Did you see those African tribe babies in the documentary? They were completely happy, and what did they have? Sticks."

So when I shared with her some excellent news—that Vincent Kovar selected me to curate and edit this monster-themed fifth volume of Gay City Anthologies—she said what any saintly mother would:

"Again with the monsters? Why do you *like* that?"

Monsters have been a bit of an obsession for me since childhood. I quickly latched onto dinosaurs, Dracula, and Audrey Two, the foul-mouthed, R&B singing, omni-gendered, flesh-eating plant from *Little Shop of Horrors*. I got in trouble at school for drawing demonic gargoyles in Spanish class. My teacher, poor Señora Gonzalez, saw them and flipped out. I was eight.

I was forbidden to watch adult horror movies, but I found my ways. When Mom was around, I got away with comedies like *Young Frankenstein* or *Haunted Honeymoon*. I even convinced her to let me watch *Killer Klowns from Outer Space*, which I then watched almost every day for what may have been years.

I don't know if that was odd, but I do know that I'm different. I always have been. I've always been fascinated by the shadows, as well as outside of typical gender—sometimes tough, sometimes pretty, often both. As a boy, I didn't want to be Batman. Cripes no. I wanted to be Catwoman, and not just any Catwoman, but Tim Burton's maniac-Michelle-Pfeiffer-S&M-Catwoman in a vinyl corset. Or one of the badass *Witches of Eastwick* (preferably nerd-turned-bombshell Susan Sarandon, though Pfeiffer and Cher also embodied the titular brides of Satan).

I learned how to be femme from monstrous women. Being able to pinball around between traditional femme and masculine presentation, combining and mixing them like glyphs in a magic incantation, gives one an edge that many people fear.

Queer people are shape-shifters. We trouble the boundaries between categories, overlapping them as often as we break them. We are clearly and effortlessly more than our bodies. Many cultures knew this and either consecrated queer people as shamans or demonized them as witches. If we can transcend the predictable body, what else might we do? We're inherently powerful and ultimately unpredictable.

Like all truly queer things, the following anthology resists tidy categorization. It's certainly not all horror, nor is it all steampunk. Stories and poems are set in the Victorian era, but also in the Great War, in the mod sci-fi 60's, and some are quite timeless. In fact, not every contributor is queer (unpredictable, indeed). From the conceptual cauldron of queerness, Victorian science fiction, ghosts, and monsters, this uproarious collection has emerged. If you've grown sleepy of LGBT genre fiction, allow this collection to reinvigorate you.

L. Frank Baum, author, filmmaker, and creator of Oz, said of fantasy, "...I believe that dreams — day dreams, you know, with your eyes wide open and your brain-matter whizzing — are likely to lead to the betterment of the world." I believe that monsters are our collective dreams, the things we fear as well as those we secretly desire. We need monsters. They crystallize the vast unknown into something we can name. Contained herein are dreams: myths, fairy tales, urban legends, and quite a few nightmares to make your brain-matter whiz and sizzle.

Our cover artist and designer, the World Fantasy Award-winning John Coulthart, no stranger to horror, has also contributed an excerpt from a novel-in-progress, a psychedelic, alchemical neo-Victorian romp that merges the styles of Burroughs and Wilde into something new and astounding. Bestselling author Dorothy Allison has gifted us with a story of lust, loss, addiction, and a saucy succubus. Lambda Award winners Jon Macy and Rebecca Brown anchor the middle of the book, Macy with his graphic fairy tale and Brown with her own essay on the monsters of her childhood.

Gregory L. Norris, ever the prolific pop wizard, brings a *Twilight Zone*-noir story about a hard-boiled actor sucked into the plot of his own show, as well as into his new co-star. Catherine Lundoff and Steve Berman, authors and editors of their own series of queer spectacular fiction anthologies, gaze into the abyss: Lundoff into the mechanical eye of the most powerful medium in London, Berman into the most brutally horrifying story in this collection, a vertigo-inducing tale of lonely bears, arrogant cannibals, meat, zombies, and bottomless hunger.

Then there are the emerging authors, people you may not have heard from before, but whom you will be hearing from again. Kat Smalley thumbs her nose at English imperialism, taking us through a steampunk India in pursuit of a robotic anarchist. Anthony Rella leads us down into the bathhouse labyrinth, where dwells—who else? The Minotaur. JL Smither remyths Achilles and Patroclus, now British soldiers in the war against the wolfmen. Amy Shepherd buys souls, while Ryan Keawekane, returning from Gay City 4, steals bodies. Also returning from volume 4 is Ryan Crawford, offering a hiker's nightmare of the Pacific Northwest.

I have insisted on the inclusion of poetry in this volume, and we've been graced with excellence. Ocean Vuong and Oscar McNary will haunt you long after you've closed the book. Imani Sims will tempt you. Jericho Brown and Janie Miller play the mad scientists, and CAConrad shows us that we were the monsters all along. Lydia Swartz takes us out of time and into a prose poetry Underworld, while Jeremy Halinen goes for the throat (and a few other vulnerable areas).

And the illustrations. My goodness. M. S. Corley provides a trio of the notorious, if coded, queer fiends from his Monsters of Literature series, while Levi Hastings has honored us with a wealth of his deliciously clever, occasionally wicked watercolors.

I am immensely proud of this book. Curating this collection has been dizzying yet sobering, like an electric shock to the loins. Ultimately, beyond the grand variety of styles, subjects, genres, and contributors, I consider this book not only coherent but also far more than the sum of its parts. A paper Frankenstein's monster, if you will.

So, to return to my long-suffering mother's loaded question, *Why do you like that?* Well, why do I like anything? Why have I seen *Alien* and *The Hunger* and *Hellraiser* dozens of times, yet I only feel compelled to see *Titanic* once?

Why do I prefer T. Rex or David Bowie, even cheesy 80's Bowie, to Lana Adele Ray Jepsen or whomever is the diva of the moment? Why am I a dog person instead of cats? Why tea over coffee, even in Seattle? Jesus' whiskers, why am I attracted to men far more than women?

Why in Hell shouldn't I adore monsters? One could do a lot worse. Monsters and the occult are a *natural* fit for those of us who've grown up accused of being "unnatural." Perhaps queers are *preter*natural, like psychics or Sasquatch, creatures eluding definition but suspected to have a "reasonable scientific explanation." We've taken back the terms "queer," "bent," and "deviant," and I fully endorse that we reappropriate the word "monster." I *am* a monster: unpredictable, disquieting, paranormal. Dreamy.

Read on.

-EJP
5/27/13
Seattle

Act I

Victorian Venom

Dr. Frankenstein's Creature

M.S. Corley

Dear Dr. Frankenstein

Jericho Brown

I, too, know the science of building men
Out of fragments in little light
Where I'll be damned if lightning don't

Strike as I forget one
May have a thief's thumb,

Another, a murderer's arm
And watch the men I've made leave
Like an idea I meant to write down,

Like a machine that works
All wrong, like the monster

God came to know the moment
Adam named animals and claimed
Eve, turning from heaven to her

As if she was his
To run. No word he said could be tamed.

No science. No design. Nothing taken
Gently into his hand or your hand or mine,
Nothing we erect is our own.

A Captive Audience

Ryan Keawekane

IT MUST BE in his hands. They were cold now, what with Winter pressed up against the studio windows like a pauper against your heels for pence. But there was a power in the hollow of the Artist's palms and intertwined between his fingers. Keeping company with Winter outside was the fog off the River Thames, which wafted up and married with the perpetual smog that her Majesty Victoria alone could rise above. For a spell, the pair would watch the Artist rub his hands together for warmth. Then, Fog would tell Winter to haunt another window, but leave the Artist alone, lest he press the soul out of Winter's bones and onto the page. But all know that Winter is a spineless fiend, and Fog a flighty companion: the former stayed to watch the Artist work as the latter flew off.

Whether the source of his power was in his hands or in the charcoal with which he drew mattered not: the Artist was an untouchable to all but the elements. He might as well be committed to a common workhouse for his abominableness.

*Work*house—hah! The poor could work all they wanted in that God-forsaken dump and never make coins enough to jingle. Still, England was a bloody dark, pitiful place, and any shelter was better than none. The poor were "offered" shelter and protection, in exchange for the sweat of their brow and the blood of their fingertips, but they suffered just the same, merely under a different oppression. The Artist was briefly one of their number, but you had to keep close quarters at all hours in those hell holes—and no one, not foreman nor pauper, not magistrate nor villain, could keep company with a man of the Artist's designs. The Artist was no longer poor—but his soul would benefit not at all from his worldly riches. The parish of this London corner had largely condemned to the pits of Hell what might remain of the Artist's soul for his "art." Yet—the Artist once but no more wondered—how can one, even a man, not revel in the beauty of the human male? And, so doing, not want to capture it on the canvas to linger *ad perpetuum*? The Artist's *designs*—his works of art, his pride, passion, and joy—were themselves a sign of still darker times to come, where men would be *allowed* to look at, observe, ponder on, and then to lust after and even touch another of the entitled sex. The Queen herself might burn the very drawings she so prized, if only she knew that those figures of men—in all their divine liberty—had been wrought by the Artist's blasphemous hands.

The Artist shook his head and nearly cut his finger. It was too cold now, and dark. But he must work tonight: the Queen was waiting. He needed a sharper pencil and, unless he wanted to paint with his own blood, he had to keep his wits about him as he whittled a point onto his drawing tool. The fire in the hearth leapt to his attention. "Here," it pled, "Warm your hands here, master!" The Artist put the whittling knife and the stick of charcoal down. Heeding the hearth's call, he turned toward the fire and put his hands out toward its lapping tongues. Yet the cold was not like soot, which could be washed off with soap and water. The cold emanated from his own bones and made a mockery of the cowardly Winter.

It must *be* in his hands. Other men had pencils and plumes, sticks of charcoal sharper than sabers. Yet none were blessed with the capability to transform living marvel into static art. For a while, no one knew about the Artist's talent, no one except for another boy named Hubert. They had been chums, boys with soot on their faces and grime in their hair. Too old for either to benefit from the State's free education mandate. Hubert was the older. The Artist, who was known then as Thomas, was like a tail to Hubert's jungle cat. They went everywhere together. They got sick together. They—grew up together. If the Artist let himself think it—and if the common prudence were to let him think it—he might think himself not fully grown until Hubert had taken Thomas into his arms. Thomas, an orphan, had been corralled into the workhouse, there to work like a cog in a clock: in cramped quarters and always turning, turning in circles and never improving his own situation.

Hubert found young Thomas, a lost soul. It was Hubert who first recognized the artist in Thomas, after their friendship had solidified into something like an arrow through the heart that neither would willingly remove. Thomas had been drawing in a pool of oil on a patch of dirty ground. It was supposed to be a face—Hubert's —but the older saw instead a cat in the lines, and Thomas let himself be so convinced. Neither could afford paper then, but it was easy enough for Hubert to squirrel some away for Thomas. He even pilfered a length of charcoal that Thomas could use as a pencil.

"Let me be your first subject," Hubert said.

And so it was. Their friendship soon became the only salve against the wounds of living. When they could steal away from the workhouse—which, while not easy, was not uncommon—the boys-becoming-men would sneak into people's homes and take a leisurely bath. Such an occasion was likely to occur on a Sunday, when parishioners of the workhouse and the neighborhood alike would come together like fingers in a fist waved at the heavens in defiance, full of malice and ungratefulness for their crummy lives all, until song and compassion would unwind some of the tension and the fist would become hands folded together in prayer. These prayers were, naturally, submitted from their separate compartments, but simultaneously. The youths would sneak out of mass and check for unlocked homes, which they always found. Absentminded Londoners were always leaving their doors unlocked, and in came the two, smelling of the chimneys they cleaned. In the dark, Hubert would search around for matchsticks to light the range. Thomas was in charge of finding the biggest pot in the kitchen and filling it up with water. Together they would carry the full pot to the stove and plop it down on the fire that Hubert had built. Then Hubert would go in search of the bathtub, which he'd bring back to the kitchen and set in front of the range. The boys would huddle down in the bathtub and wait for the water to boil. The two were old for chimneysweepers, but they could almost fit into the same pair of trousers, they were so thin. Gangly, they were, though Hubert was broadening out already. Each boy collected his knees in an embrace to wait and think. Thomas would look into the cold, empty kitchen hearth, wishing for the warmth of a real fire. It was always cold in London: either *dry and* or *wet and*.

If it wasn't the hearth Thomas was looking at, it was Hubert. Hubert was really turning into a man. His face was thinning out, eyes more tired, lips thinner. He had a beard coming in but no hope for a razor to shave it when it got too long. There was something about his shoulders, too. Hubert was banging into things more often, even getting stuck in the flue. Thomas was sorry and afraid that Hubert would have to change professions soon. But Hubert was also becoming something else that Thomas couldn't yet describe. Recognition of that something was always accompanied by a pang in Thomas' heart. Thomas would feel an ache in his chest if Hubert should touch his hand.

They sat in the bathtub, the two of them, thinking their thoughts, until the water had boiled. Thomas would long for a pencil and paper to capture the moment on, above all the soulfulness in Hubert's distant gaze. Even until now, the sound of water boiling made the Artist's blood run hot. When the water had boiled, Hubert would ask, "Do you have the soap?" and Thomas would go racing off into the blue-tinged dark toward the bedroom where the soap was usually hidden. He took his time returning. By the time they had stolen baths from five homes, Thomas knew what to expect upon returning to the bathtub.

The stove fire was the only source of illumination in the small, cozy house, but from the living area Thomas could see Hubert's silhouette. Thomas had left a boy in dirty rags and heavy boots, soles wearing thin. Returning, Thomas found a nude man, standing over the bathtub, eyes on the emptiness therein, mind a-wander. In the darkness, Thomas dared not breathe. The lines of Hubert's body were perfect: long and unbroken, they glowed with the blue firelight off the range, which trembled in time with the whipping winds outside. Or was that Hubert's heartbeat, thudding just beneath his pale, pale skin? He was all bones, but sinewy muscle, too, taut even at his most relaxed. His hair touched his shoulders, a dark chestnut, like wings of a falcon, and his nose had the likeness of the bird's beak: sharply hooked but wide at the base. Thomas could stand there for entire minutes, studying Hubert's physical design, but never looking at *him*. In the periphery of his vision, Thomas saw Hubert, saw *him* there without a will of *his* own—but Thomas had will enough for them two. He dared not look at that flesh and want for it to come to life. He was young, but he knew things about himself, about Hubert. He knew that he must not have these sorts of feelings, though he couldn't know how he knew. One doesn't entertain feelings of any sort of sexual nature in Victoria's England. Thomas was young but old enough to know what he knew, and to know that he wanted sorely to know Hubert more, whatever consequences might befall his soul later.

The air in the room would change and Hubert would realize that Thomas had not returned. When their eyes met from either side of the thick, syrupy darkness, the older would smile half a smile and call the younger over.

Then, they would both work the buttons on Thomas' clothes open and pull off his boots. Standing naked, the boys would put three cups of hot boiling water for every two cups of cold into the tub until it was halfway full. The older might adjust the temperature as he saw fit. Thomas was always the first to get in and, standing over him, Hubert would ladle the warm-hot water over the younger. Sometimes, Thomas would *see* Hubert and, unable to look away, just stare at *him*. It was bigger all the time, with a tufty shawl around the base that was wiry, and nothing at all like feathers, though there was something avian about this aspect of Hubert's anatomy, too. Sometimes, Hubert would talk, to himself mostly, since Thomas, struck dumb, never could keep much conversation. Finally, when Thomas was all wet except for his head, which they would wash last, Hubert would wipe his feet off and step gingerly into the tub. The water level would rise up to almost Thomas' shoulders, and the younger would feel an ugly, debilitating aching in this stomach. His limbs refused to work. Hubert would interpret the boy's lassitude for exhaustion or malnourishment and take the rag he carried with him everywhere out of the pocket of his overalls and, with the soapstone, work up a decent lather, which he'd spread like a thin paste all over Thomas' skin. This was not the gesture of one washing another. It was the gesture of a baker basting prized bread and, by the look in Hubert's eyes, the baker was hungry.

The door to the studio flew open, and Winter swooped down into the hearth and stole all the warmth away from the Artist's fingers, which were only beginning to regain their utility. Three men came in, dragging a boy and a woman in with them. The tallest of the men, a wreath of black around his crooked mouth, slammed the door shut, and Winter's cries of agony grew distant, leaving behind a ragged howling that characterized the months of December and January. The boy was breathing deeply, terror-stricken, but the woman was deathly silent, her face beaten.

"What shall we do with the boy?" Blackbeard asked.

"Strip him," said the Artist without lifting his gaze from his hands.

The two that had dragged the woman in deposited her on the chair in the corner, where she sat, free to struggle toward freedom but without the will. The three then stripped the clothes off the young man. He whimpered some but put up no fight. The only additional sound the boy made was when they pulled his undershirt and night pants off: a sharp intake of air, as of surprise. The boy was anatomically a man. The lines of his body reminded the Artist of a faraway night in a not-so-distant place—and a bathtub. When the boy was

16

naked, the three men backed away, wary of being between model and artist. All but Blackbeard and the Artist were breathing shallow breaths, as if through a straw, lungs never fully satisfied. The lackeys exchanged glances, rubbing their hands together anxiously.

The Artist felt a pang of disgust. "Wait outside," he ordered them. When they were gone, the Artist told Blackbeard to tie the woman up. Blackbeard sat the boy's mother up in the chair and bound her hands and feet. He stripped the bonnet from her head, because it reminded the Artist of the mourning Victoria. The Queen made him uneasy, because she was powerful woman and because he knew that she could end him—life and career—if she knew that the male nudes she so adored weren't *interpretations* of life but life *itself*, wrested into the canvas by his hands. It must be in his *hands*!

Pious Queen Victoria fancied the naked male figure and paid a pretty penny for the Artist's designs. The female form was golden but, like such intentions, it paved the way to Hell. That of a man, however... The slight musculature and build of a healthy male was an apt personification of the Queen's England: broad of shoulder, fine of hand, handsome of face, long and powerful of limb. The empire was flourishing under her command, even though her heart had died with Prince Albert almost three decades hence. Albert had shared his Queen's fancy for the drawn male form; she had even gifted him one of the Artist's best renderings of a man by the name of Louis Humboldt who'd owned a farm on the outskirts of Paris. The bank had come to collect the mortgage on this farm but Humboldt could not afford to pay it. He agreed to model for the Artist. In exchange the Artist would use a portion of the Queen's fee to pay off the farmer's account. The Artist cared not that the man had a wife, some seven children, and most undoubtedly a mistress and yet more illegitimate brats to his name. The Artist was moved, however, by Humboldt's handsomeness. The model was tall and fair-haired with a clearly English bearing, tint, and refinement, despite being an established French citizen.

This recollection soured the Artist's mood. The French and English alike were enjoying a time of plenty and effervescence. The so-called *Belle Époque* had just begun and was poised to catch up with the British Empire's *Victorian Era*, already well underway. But Victoria, the Artist's only remaining admirer, already had in mind a photographer to capture her *memento mori*, a chap named Sullivan whose retinue was large but whose craft was more pomp than circumstance. The Queen would assume her final position and, so

17

immortalized, join Albert in the grave. And with her, the Artist's fees would become as memory: intangible and unreliable.

Fog and Winter had enlisted a third companion, it seemed, who came knocking on the Artist's door: Nostalgia. It blurred the lines between the moment at hand and the past. Here, the lascivious and unfaithful hearth fire licked Blackbeard's cheeks and, at an angle and depending on the fire's tongue, it reminded the Artist of chimney soot, a perpetual mark on his soul. Soot got in everything. The youths Thomas and Hubert would wash their hands and their feet before going to bed, adding their worn and weary bodies to the steaming mass of sleeping men. But it was hard to wash the soot and grime out of their stinking heads.

On that night, which stood out among the clearest in all of the Artist's recollection, Hubert and Thomas washed their bodies off with the soapstone, the water quickly turning to ink. But the water would retain its heat for a long while, so the grime had occasion to cling to their skin again and be washed off again. Hubert's eyes were distant. Thomas imagined that Hubert was wishing after a girl that he fancied. He was old enough to bed a girl and there was always one or two lasses offering evil services in hushed tones, but these young men couldn't be bothered. Thomas often wondered if, perhaps, Hubert didn't want to be bothered by a sticky wench, especially when the cold tendrils of winter slithered between their shivering bodies and froze parts of them solid. Asleep, the two would press together, like matchsticks, Thomas full of phosphorescence enough to burn them all if Hubert should stoke the tinder of his own lust. Sometimes, exhausted but bothered, some of the men would touch themselves, and others. It was a desperate time, and women were expensive. Thomas dared not touch himself. But when winter was among them, twisting them into themselves, Thomas would put his ever-frozen hands between their two bodies and find Hubert *awake* and cold but growing warmer all the time. Rather than melt, however, Hubert's erection would throb at its hardest. They were in their bedclothes, which were of thin material. If the sleep come to claim Hubert was feeble, he would thrust himself between Thomas' hands, working his hips like slow, jerky pistons. Hubert would whimper pathetically and hide his face against Thomas' neck, all the while "sleeping." Thomas, too, but he kept his hands stationary, holding the flimsy material encasing Hubert lightly in his hands, so that he could slip and slide freely, until the passion flooded between them. In the morning, Hubert would wake early to wash his soiled pants. Thomas would find him freezing, huddled in a corner, bed shirt covering everything but his head, his wet pants hanging on a hook to freeze dry. Thomas would squat down beside him, and they would huddle together for warmth. Sometimes, one or the other would cry with the same pitifulness that had consumed them the night before.

The boy sobbing stirred the Artist and brought him back to center. Blackbeard was standing the boy beside the studio hearth, which was bigger than the kitchen's, warmer and brighter as well. Shaking off Nostalgia, the Artist returned to his work. After rubbing his forefinger and thumb against the charcoal, the Artist smeared a rough impression of the boy's outline onto the page. Blackbeard came to lean over the Artist's shoulder and examine his technique.

"The first thing to capture," said the Artist, "is his willpower. Put that on the page first, and you can take your time getting the rest of him right. His body will long for reunion with his soul, and the work is easier thus." When the smudge was complete, it had the vague outline of a young male, but it could have been a tall building through the pea soup, or a limbless tree. The boy, with hair touching his shoulders and a familiar nose, reminded the Artist of Hubert, and he was filled with disgusting desire.

"Wake the woman!" he snapped in anger.

The mother had sobbed herself to sleep, and Blackbeard slapped her in the face to wake her. When that didn't work, he took a cup of cold water and doused her with it. She awoke with a start and an intake of breath, almost choking. She was disoriented for a moment, until she saw her son standing perfectly still beside the fireplace, bathed in its golden glow. Then she remembered the situation and let loose a shriek. Blackbeard slapped her again, and the sound went out of her.

"Don't quiet her," the Artist ordered. "I need her pain."

So Blackbeard shook her, forced her eyes open when she tried to close them, kept her head in place so she couldn't turn away, tortured her when she had numbed. The boy stood by the fireplace, silhouetted by orange firelight, a puppet on the end of the Artist's string. He had ceased sobbing. His eyes were fixed on a faraway place, following the arc his soul drew through the ether without moving his gaze off the Artist's easel. In a distant memory, Thomas and Hubert were huddled in the dark corner of a room full of uncomfortable, lumpy beds, conveyances to the dream realm for a hundred lumpy heads. The Artist brought his charcoal to the paper canvas: a stroke right down the middle of the page to capture the spine. He needed to design a framework upon which to hang the youth's muscle, bones, and skin. The smudge of soul on the page writhed under the pencil tip, but the boy—soulless—moved not. Onto the vertical spine the Artist hung the torso, which would house the heart, lungs, diaphragm, stomach, and entrails. Beneath, the Artist traced a circle to suggest the boy's pelvis, the curve of his hips, which were narrow but expanding with maturity. Then, sticks parallel to the boy's living limbs were drawn on the paper, dark and heavy. Calves, ankles, and feet were implied by bulbs and hooks on and at the end of the "legs." Next, the shoulders, drawn back to spread wide the pectorals, though the youth's chest was still narrow. A line on either side of the "torso" suggested the arms, which hung at the boy's side. The Artist appraised his marionette and wished he had had the chance to so ensorcell his beloved Hubert.

"How...?" Blackbeard asked, never finishing the question. He had seen this before but couldn't understand the power the Artist exercised over his victims. In this room—indeed, in this quarter—they whispered not of the Ripper, the nameless serial killer that frequented Whitechapel's alleys, but of the Artist, whom some called the Vanisher.

"If I knew, would you expect me to tell you?"

"So even you dare not recognize your own...monstrosity?"

The Artist's eyes found Blackbeard's. He might have felt ire but he was filled instead with realization: He was coming to be seen as he saw himself, too. And so the enlightening had begun...

"You think me a *monster*?" he asked Blackbeard.

"I think you a master, but one with certain...evil qualities."

"You think me evil?"

"I think you generous and—"

"Oh, come off the sniveling!" the Artist snapped. "Bare your thoughts, man. Do you or do you not think me a monster?"

"I think not. I only fear you as a monster wishes to be feared."

The Artist nodded. It was true. Fear was fodder for the monstrous, so the Artist was a monster. Glancing at the boy's mother, the Artist sneered. Society had designated woman house-maker: to cook the meals, tend to the children, keep the house in order. In most ways, the Artist had no need of a woman, any woman—even the Queen. What he needed in the Queen was a heavily padded clientele. Likewise, what he needed in this boy's mother was her pain, and fear was a necessary tinder for said. They went well together: fear and pain. The boy would feel neither, so his mother should feel enough for them both. She need not make the Artist's bed or tend to his hearth, but the mother would prepare a feast of fear for him and he would be satisfied. For a time.

"Hubert?" he called out, and the boy raised his head.

"Thomas," answered the boy. The youth's mouth moved in response, but Blackbeard could see the creases at the Artist's temples, the tension working in the master's jaw. The lackey wondered what kind of power this was and how the Artist came to possess it.

The Artist said, "You left me, Hubert."

"Yes," answered the boy. "I'm sorry, Thomas."

"You abandoned me."

"Yes, but not of my own volition. I should like to have stayed forever…"

The boy's mother writhed against her bindings and spat at the Artist. "Why are you doing this? He's my son!"

Blackbeard smacked her full across the face and she and her chair were toppled over. When the tall one had righted the chair, a streak of blood had appeared at the corner of her mouth. A lunacy, silent and smoldering, had entered her eyes, too. Blackbeard hovered over her, looked her square in the eyes, and she began to holler for help.

The boy said, "They can't help you, mother. No one can."

The mother wailed with even more force. "Why are you doing this, you monster?!" she cried at the Artist and down she went again, having collided with Blackbeard's open palm.

"Enough," the Artist said, and Blackbeard righted the woman's chair again.

"I'm not your son," said the boy to his mother.

"What?" she blathered.

"I am not your son. My name is Hubert. Thomas and I share a bond. We are—more than friends…" The boy's voice took on an eerie quality that no human voice could, mechanical and gritty.

The woman ceased wailing and began to sob. But her pitifulness was delicious! The Artist felt the disgust in his gut dissipate, burnt to nothing by passion of a truer, more genuine kind: art! He brought his hands to the canvas, rested the charcoal against the white, and began to tear the boy out of the living realm and into—what? Even the Artist knew not where the captured went. They vanished everywhere but on the page. The Artist drew dark, heavy lines that would have cut through lighter stationery. He would save the boy's face, his head, until the end. The first to be captured was always the genitals. It was paramount that these go first, while his passion for *art* was fueled by the model's mother's cries. And this was also the point in the night when her cries were strongest, most piteous, most pathetic. It stoked his passion many times over. *Hubert* had been bigger than tonight's boy, but they were both more men than boys, in this regard. The Artist captured the boy's genitals on the page in thick strokes, all the while the boy made pathetic noises in his throat that emanated out his nose. The youth whimpered, but his eyes were lifeless. Perhaps they were seeing the beyond into which he was being drawn. If so, it mustn't be a decent place: his whimpering was pitiful. This was the noise that Hubert had made at night when the winter cold would wind him and Thomas into a wicked embrace. The boy's voice was Hubert's, but the mother's was all her own—and she sobbed and moaned and groaned and cried that it would be over, that the Artist would take her soul but not her son's, that Blackbeard would kill her now! But the Artist needed her pain. He *lived* on it, bread and butter.

During those moments, when the Artist was wrestling a model into the canvas, Hubert was temporarily revived, and Thomas the man was forced to relive the past.

Hubert had been transferred out of the collective of chimneysweepers when his size became a detriment. He became a collier, forced to drag corves of coal out of the mines. He had been forced to live in another quarter, away from his beloved Thomas, and the winter they spent apart was evilest to the younger, who could befriend no other in Hubert's absence. Thomas was waiting for the colliers to call his number, but Hubert didn't have it in him to hold out. Thomas ran away from the workhouse when he found out about Hubert's death. Thomas dared not go back. He expected to die on the streets of London, but he proved a smart youth and hardworking. In many ways, he was already a man. He begged on the streets for a while, until he had become good enough at drawing to create products worth selling.

Eventually, young Thomas came into the company of a true artist. His name was Wilhelm, and no one liked him because he was a foreigner, but Thomas found him a decent fellow. They both preferred the friendship of none, and so provided each other perfect company. At first, Thomas was secretive. He would hide his artistic abilities, because they were feeble beside Wilhelm's. But the man never judged him. Wilhelm was a bright fellow whose only and ultimate mistake in life would be befriending Thomas. And here is where the foreigner exercised the height of his infirmity. He couldn't know, and neither could Thomas—who had seen in Hubert the perfect subject—that volunteering to be the Artist's subject would be Wilhelm's final profession.

Wilhelm asked Thomas if he would prefer a nude model. Thomas only nodded. Wilhelm understood something of Thomas' need to befriend men. But Wilhelm was a womanizer of the most absolute sense: he bedded them, then threw them away. Aside from those lust-filled moments, Wilhelm readily shared all others with Thomas, so naturally the boy had seen him in every possible regard. Assuming a comfortable pose, Wilhelm sat on his divan, nude as God intended. Thomas had seen *him* before, but had not looked so intently. "Get your fill," Wilhelm said in jest. Thomas tried to hide his shame and scorn, but failed pathetically. Thomas leveled his pencil on the paper and lasciviously applied himself to capturing *Wilhelm* on the page. The artist became so swept up in his own bliss that he didn't recognize the discomfort consuming his subject.

"What are you doing?" asked Wilhelm with a constricted throat. He was writhing on the divan in a mixture of lust and disgust.

"Drawing you," Thomas said simply.

"But *how?*"

"With a pencil." Thomas continued. He had not yet the technique of plotting out his subject's stature, of hanging the limbs on the framework. Wilhelm's genitalia floated in the middle of the page, faint but growing darker, heavier, fuller with each stroke of the youth's pencil. They might have been exotic fruits—or a flower, stamen hanging down between two round, bulbous petals lightly dusted.

"Stop that!" Wilhelm cried, reaching for his trousers. But the strength had gone out of his legs, and he couldn't raise himself off the divan. "Thomas, what is this wickedness? I have no strength in my legs and the sensation in my loins is terrible!"

"I don't know," said the artist honestly.

"What did you draw?"

Shame-faced, Thomas showed Wilhelm the voluptuous lines he had used to capture the elder's sex.

"Erase it!" Wilhelm ordered.

Thomas tried to erase it. But the sensation put life into Wilhelm's loins, and the stamen stood to attention, stroked to ecstasy by Thomas' eraser. "Shall I stop?" Thomas asked, seeing the frustrated desire on his model's face.

Wilhelm stammered something unintelligible but didn't ask the boy to stay his hand. The older was thoroughly enjoying the terrible sensation delivered by Thomas' eraser, so, thought Thomas, what kind of ecstasy must be had at the *tip* of the pencil? Wilhelm's eyes closed, mouth agape, he couldn't see that Thomas had repositioned his pencil and was drawing strokes on the page. "Stop…" the subject murmured, but in the air between them the plea was transformed into a prayer to continue.

When Thomas was not looking, Wilhelm's pleasure gave way to a kind of pain, and he became slave to the young man's charcoal. An artist was being born even as the gloaming claimed the day and wrapped it in autumnal colors. The Artist saw his subject Wilhelm but wasn't *seeing* him. There was a sense of manipulation between his fingers, at the tip of his pencil—which had become a sword, cutting the life right out of the older gentleman. When Thomas the Artist was done, Wilhelm and any trace of his bodily existence were gone, but the haunting quality of his gaze was trapped on the page, the agape mouth moving within the confines of the second dimension. All of Wilhelm was there, nude, but the desire had gone out of him like the flame of an exposed candle. Somewhere, the passion had claimed them both, and Wilhelm, thus borne to the other side of ecstasy, had surrendered to it. Thomas, however, was still full of desire and abandoned himself to the whims of his free hand.

The Artist had captured his first audience, pressing the third dimension flat into two. He kept Wilhelm forever close to his heart, his bed, his hand, and ever at the back of his mind as his first *chef-d'oeuvre*. There were many others. Subjects all, and male to boot, they were plucked up out of reality and dumped ceremoniously onto the page, as leaves raked together in a pile. Eventually, the throes of life would dissipate from their flattened forms and the Artist would grow frustrated again. He stalked the dark alleys for more models until the renown of his pieces could no longer be ignored. He came into the Queen's interest this way, not accidentally as history would later retell. The Queen learned his name well upon first sight of one of his nudes. By then, he had shed the trifling skin of a pitiable orphan named Thomas and took the moniker "the Artist" which, the desired effect achieved, implied that none else on the face of the earth merited the title. He was the one and only artist.

A shriek in the night brought the Artist back from the past again: the subject's mother was gawking at the spot where her son used to be. All that remained of the almost-man was the vague impression of a shadow's shade. "You vanished him!" she cried.

The Artist beat Nostalgia back with his pencil and refocused on the page. There, he found Hubert's latest incarnation—ecstasy, frustration, and resignation all enveloped in the youth's flesh. "Speak," he ordered it.

"What shall I say?" came the metallic voice from the other side.

"Tell me of your fear."

"I am afraid, master."

"Tell me of your lust."

"I am so filled, master."

The mother cried, "Stop!" but artist and subject continued their macabre dialogue.

"Tell me of the other side," the Artist ordered.

"It is ecstasy here," moaned the subject voluptuously. "All your subjects await you, for reunion with he who captured us here. Your audience awaits, master."

"Your wait shall be delicious and, like a magnificent sweet, take time to rightly savor!" With a few final strokes, the Artist consummated the piece and the shadow against the hearth was reunited with its caster on the Artist's canvas. They embraced. The Artist gave Blackbeard the word. Thus consigned, Blackbeard wrung the life out of the subject's mother, who gave one final shriek before her light went out. Blackbeard called to his men who came to clean up the mess. As the two dragged the woman's corpse out, Blackbeard could not keep himself from asking the Artist, "That voice, coming through the boy... Was it yours?"

"It was Hubert's," answered the Artist.

"From the other side, you mean?"

"You could say that. But part of him is still with us. In me." In the firelight, he gazed at his hands and felt the power coursing through them. He knew where his power came from. It only made sense now! With a dark snicker, he thanked Hubert silently for this gift. The two one day would be reunited, and only then would Hubert's gift be returned to Hubert himself, and Thomas could thank him in person, in words and gestures. Thomas would put his hands on Hubert and exercise sorcery of a wholly different sort on him.

Leaving his henchmen to clean up the studio, the Artist stole into the cold and dark toward his only client and her heavy wallet. An icy rain was falling, the diamond pellets striking his face and ricocheting away. The Artist didn't flinch: pain of the body was a welcome detachment. He hoped wistfully that the Queen should be satisfied with his offering and fill his purse and heart both with change, though he knew, no matter the quantity, it would never be enough for the Artist to give up his profession. He would continue this employment until his death, exacted by the hands of a would-be victim. But this wintry night, in his hands he held a power that not even Her Majesty, from the loftiness of the throne, could fully perceive. The Artist's hands possessed a power held by no one before and never again after. But let the Queen live long and prosperously without ever knowing the terror his hands were capable of! Long live Victoria, Queen of England!

Dorian Gray
M.S. Corley

Medium Méchanique

Catherine Lundoff

I DID NOT know the others seated around the table, their faces dim in the flickering of the gaslight. Since we had not been introduced, it would have been impossible for me, an unchaperoned, but seemingly respectable young lady, to speak to either of the two gentlemen. As for the three other women, respectable or otherwise, none met my eyes and I did not try hard to meet theirs.

So we were resigned to wait for Madame LaFarge in near silence, broken only by the soft whispers of the man and the woman who sat on my right and the occasional popping noise from the lights. These sounds were accompanied by the rustling of silk as the lady in the green dress of that fabric removed her gloves and craned her neck around to look at the room, the ceiling and, unsurprisingly, the door.

Since she was seated across the table from me, I was able to watch her fidgets unobstructed. She was clearly not respectable, or not as was judged so in Her Majesty's England of 1888, where steam-powered carriages filled London's streets, but a certain kind of woman might be killed with impunity in Whitechapel. A bit less silk, a bit less elegance, and she might have joined their numbers.

In another life, I would have wondered why she or, indeed, any of them, were here. Not everyone likes what they hear when they ask to speak with the dead, or so I had been told by those who claimed to know. I suspected that I would not. Yet I stayed. Perhaps Madame would not prove a charlatan like the others I had visited. Maybe Annabel would indeed speak to me through her tonight, saying the things I longed to hear.

I did not care if the others heard those things as well, thereby proving that I, too, was not respectable.

My thoughts turned to the chance acquaintance who had sent me here with tales of a medium who was so close to the spirit world she seemed to dwell there herself. The woman had shuddered when she spoke of Madame and her mechanical eye, until I wondered if she shuddered more at the eye than anything she claimed to have heard.

But I had not credited her talk of unknown terrors and mysterious voices. I cared only that she said that Madame was able to speak with the spirits, unlike the others I had seen. That was enough for me.

My quest had brought me here to these shabby rented rooms near the Thames. I could smell the river from my chair, its scent roaming the city streets as it rode the back of the ever-present fog. They had said that the fog would vanish when all the open fires were replaced with engines and steam, but so far, that had not proved the case. The air remained thick whenever the air was still, though it did not settle for days at a time, as it had when Annabel and I each arrived here by our separate paths. How long ago that seemed!

It must have shown on my face: that terrible longing, the pain that I could barely endure. The lady on my left side reached over to squeeze my hand and broke her silence to murmur something, a phrase that might have been comfort. Or something else entirely. I summoned a tremulous smile of thanks, but gave only a cursory glance at her aging face beneath its black veil. It was not her I had come to see.

That was the moment when Madame LaFarge entered the room, and with her came the chill of purest winter, though the weather outside was autumnal and mild. I felt the cold run so deep run through me that I feared that I might never move again. Not the pure clean cold of a winter's sleigh ride this, but a freeze that made me think of one of Dante's Hells. Or the grave.

The lady on my left withdrew her hand to press it to her mouth, holding back the exclamation that she was too well-bred to utter. Madame turned her head, shifting her mechanical eye one way, then the other, as she watched our faces. The maid following at her heels turned up the gas stove in the corner, then turned down the gaslights, casting the room into shadow before she left. All the while, Madame's mechanical eye whirred with a life all its own, glowing pale blue in its Stygian depths.

If I had been able to command my limbs, I might have screamed and fled. I, who had spoken out for women's suffrage to an angry mob, I who was able to face the death of my heart's companion and the ignominy of being cast from my father's house and yet survive, nearly fell captive to my own terrors. But what would Annabel think of me, if indeed she could see me at all?

And Annabel seeing me, to one extent or another, was why I had come. I twisted my hands together until my knuckles ached under the worn kid of my gloves, fighting for control. To distract myself, I thought about the small pistol in my clutch, brought for defense, or for afterward, when this medium failed as the others had before her. I had decided that when that happened, there would be no more need for defense or mediums.

But perhaps she would not fail. I risked another glance at her face.

Madame had a human eye to accompany the other, its muddy brown rendering it nearly invisible when contrasted to the whirring gears and spectral glow of its mate. Yet when it met mine, I found it in me to shudder. This was the eye of a woman who saw beyond the world we dwell in, a woman who knew the spirit world the way an ordinary mortal might know her garden.

In that moment, I wanted to believe most fervently in Madame LaFarge's powers. In that moment, I had no further plans for the pistol except that it would pointed away from me if I needed to fire it. I would give all that I had left to ensure that Madame would not call me from the beyond to a room such as this, to face either eye again.

She released me after a moment, abandoning me to the cold and the terror while she studied each of the others in turn. The woman in green silk gasped at what she saw in that face and pressed her hands to her mouth, eyes wide in shock. Then she rose from her seat, looking away from those terrible eyes. Her complexion was ashen and her hands trembled as if she had an ague. In a moment, her skirts and hat were gathered and she was gone, leaving behind her an empty space that felt even colder than before.

Madame LaFarge sat down and became a small woman in a blue silk turban, her hands large and long-fingered, her face below those eyes slack and dull like a sculptor's putty. Her dress was exotic, composed as it was of a turban, a tunic and a full skirt, with silk scarves fluttering at neck and waist.

"Good evening." The voice that welled out between those thin lips was too large for so small a woman. I wondered if it was her own, imagining for an instant that she was controlled like a ventriloquist's dummy by someone in another room. Or perhaps by whatever lurked in the blue glowing depths of her mechanical eye.

Then she smiled at us and I dropped my gaze to the table, determined to see that face no more for a time. "All of you have come here to speak to spirits who have gone on: fathers, brothers, lovers," I could feel her gaze weigh on my bent head and I bit back a gasp of horror at having my secret revealed. Madame continued speaking but I was lost for an eternity until I could drag myself thought over thought back to the sound of her voice and the darkened room.

"—be quite sure. I am not a charlatan. Are you prepared for what may come when I call? It will not be what you are expecting. Of that you may be sure." She looked at each of us again in turn, this time longest at the man and woman at my side. He stood, though she clutched his arm, and held his hand out to help her rise. His lips were tight with a terrible resolve; I did not think her pleas could move him.

And at last, head bent and shoulders drooping, she did as he wished. He bowed slightly to us, then, taking his wife by the arm, towed her from the room.

And now we were three. Madame smiled to see us still sitting there, waiting on her pleasure. "You are all certain. Good. Please move closer so that you are each seated next to each other."

No power on Earth would persuade me to move closer to her, to cross the abyss of the two empty chairs that shielded me. So I vowed. I prayed fervently to a Heaven I no longer believed in when her mechanical eye focused on me. Its cold blue light called me like a distant star, or the voice of a faraway demon. I rose as if on strings, moved closer to her, and sat as I was bidden.

Madame continued, "Now we will begin. Place your hands upon the table, your fingers touching those of the person next to you." My hands rose to the table of their own accord, fingers outstretched. A part of my mind noticed that I no longer wore my gloves and I wondered when I had taken them off.

The lady on my left trembled out to the length of her fingertips. I could feel her fear when our cold fingers touched. Part of me admired her courage for remaining here in the face of such terror, while another part of me thought her a fool, and myself as well, for failing to follow the example of our fellows and fleeing this dark room full of unseen dead things.

On my right, my fingers touched those of Madame LaFarge, my flesh cringing from the cold dampness of her outlandishly long fingers. They were the hands of a strangler, as Annabel might have said when she was reading one of her penny-dreadfuls aloud to me. I shivered harder at the thought.

Would Annabel come here tonight? And if she did, what might she say to me? Would she know about the pistol, the blackness of my thoughts these last months? Would she wish to haunt my loneliness with more than her memory?

Madame's flesh was gray in the gaslight and looking at it, I thought that perhaps my pistol was a surer route of seeing Annabel again.

There came then a distant sound of rhythmical thumping, as if someone played upon a drum in a nearby room. A sharp, sweet smell filled the air, wafting in from outside. *Incense*, my mind recognized it a moment later. Was Madame then a woman who kept Sabbath and a pew of her own, perhaps in a church nearby? I could not see her as such, not she with that hellish mechanical eye of hers. It would terrify the other devout.

The drumming caught me up as the incense settled like a cloud upon the room. I could no longer smell the Thames, which was a blessing. Instead, I inhaled the sweet scent deeply, letting myself drift upon the heavy air while I waited to see what Madame would do next. With no small part of my mind, I hoped that she might do nothing at all.

But I watched her to find out. Slowly, her mortal eye closed and the light dimmed in her mechanical one, and she tilted her head back. Her profile brought a hawk to mind and I tried without success to stop imagining her swooping down upon her clients and seizing them in her claws. If anything, her fingers against mine grew even icier and the room with them, and her breath the wind that blew ice shards against my cheeks.

There was a quiet hum filling my ears now, louder even than the drums or the small gasps and labored breathing of my companions. The sound overrode even the pounding of my own heart in my ears, and soon I could hear nothing else.

I do not know how long we sat in that sepulchral cold and sound, breathing no air not laden with incense, hearing no sound but the humming and the drum, but it felt as if hours passed before Madame spoke. I was surprised to find my eyes closed, tightly sealed as if I could not bear to see any more of my surroundings. I did not open them at first. Her words ended the humming and the now much fainter sound of the drum. "Hello? Who is there? I can feel you nearby. Do you wish to speak to someone here?"

Hers was the tone of a governess or a nursemaid. I wondered if the dead responded like guilty children caught stealing cookies when Cook's back was turned.

Then I bethought me of Annabel. I remembered her eyes, dark as a moonlit sea, and her skin like damask. But most of all I remembered her laughter: girlish and pealing. I could not hear her laugh without joining in. *Please, love, come to me. Tell me that you still love me.* Even now, in my own thoughts, I could not bring myself to ask what I really wanted to know. What would I do if she said no? I did not wonder what would happen if she said nothing at all. Instead, I opened my eyes reluctantly to see what the medium might do next.

Madame's thin lips parted in a whisper that turned to a dull growl that resonated through my bones. I heard the gentleman seated across from me gasp, his eyes gleaming white in the flickering gaslight. His mouth opened and he drank the thick air in gulps like a fish, or one drowning. The growling whisper from Madame's lips was meant for him and him alone, though we heard some words: "Betrayal. Money. Vengeance."

The gentleman stared at Madame until his eyes nearly bulged. I wondered who he had betrayed and why. I wondered what the vengeance would be. But I did not wonder much or strongly as I might have done before I entered Madame's rooms. It was as if I watched from a great distance, somewhere far above the room and its inhabitants. To my relief, I could barely hear her voice from there.

The cold grew worse and something began to form in the smoky air. It was pale and wore no shape that I could recognize. But then, it had not come for me. The gentleman pulled his hands from the table and started to his feet. His gaze was fixed on the shape, whatever it was, and he was pale, paler than Annabel was on her deathbed. His hands trembled as he reached into his pocket.

Madame whispered, "Come!" And the shape drifted forward, not quite so formless now. There was a suggestion of features in it: hands, eyes, a man's arms.

The gentleman stepped back, a flash of something sharp in his hand. "Stay back! Call him off!" This last was said to Madame, who watched him with her mechanical eye. There was a hint of a smile twisting her lips.

My other hand was aching and when I looked down, I realized that the lady next to me was holding onto me, her grip rigid and tight as iron bands. A cry from the man brought my gaze back up and I gasped to see the tableau before us. The gentleman was struggling with something, a formless thing now formed, its fingers locked around his throat.

His hand flashed once, twice. I could see the blade gleam and emerge unblemished, having cut nothing. His arms flailed, dropping the knife and he kicked out once, twice, before he fell to the carpet. I could not bring myself to stand and see how it would end. Instead, I closed my eyes like a coward and waited for his struggles to subside.

There came only silence and a long indrawn breath, one laden with satisfaction. Madame's. I wondered what was next for us and forced my eyes open. The incense was so thick now I could scarce see the room around us and my eyes burned with it. I closed them again and tried to use my other senses. Strain as I might, I could hear no sound until Madame raised her hands and clapped them slowly.

It must have been a signal of some kind because the cloud began to gradually recede, leaving the cold behind like a blanket. I opened my eyes, and across from us, sat the gentleman, seemingly undamaged by his travails. But he had the pallor of the long dead, though I could hear him breathe. He met my eyes for a moment and I shuddered as I turned away, unwilling to think too much on what I saw there.

Had I imagined his fall, spectral fingers at his throat? Why would I have imagined such a thing? The room spun around me for an instant and I could feel myself becoming faint. Madame's grip caught my hand, pulling me back. "Do not leave the circle. The spirits are not done with us yet." Her lips turned up in a smile so dreadful that I feared I might go mad.

And then it all changed. Madame's look became merely sardonic, her mechanical eye examining, then dismissing me. The lady at my side loosened her hold on my aching fingers, and the gentleman, when I looked again, seemed no more than the normal wintery pale of a Londoner kept too long inside.

Was I going mad? I heard Annabel's laughter from far away, but it had a mocking quality that she had never had in life. Was she going to come to us next? I felt ill at the thought. What if what came was no longer Annabel as I had loved her?

The drumming had begun anew, though it might have begun far earlier than that for all I knew, while my thoughts whirled and I was lost in my fears. Now I stared around wildly, determined to miss nothing. I would not lose myself in the incense or the monotonous sounds, not this time! The cold would be my friend and help me stay alert.

Madame's mechanical eye fixed upon the lady at my side this time. I heard a small, animal sound from the lady's throat, but she showed no other sign of distress. I could not read her face behind her veil but she did not seize my hand again and her fingers did not tremble where they lay against mine. I sent a small prayer that whoever she wanted speech with meant her no harm. I did not think I could bear to sit through such an attack again.

If indeed I had sat through it the first time.

I felt ill and faint at the thought. Always, I had prized my reason above all else. If that were gone, what now had I left?

The air had clouded while I was lost in my terror, and despite myself, I let it begin to overwhelm my senses. Madame's head rolled on her shoulders, mortal eye showing white around the edges, and I tried to prepare myself for what might come next.

"Are you there? Who have you come to speak to?" Madame's voice was louder now, as if she had less to fear by speaking in her normal voice. Perhaps she did. The table rocked beneath our hands as if the ocean ran beneath it and I bit back a scream at the unexpected movement. It rose and hovered for a moment and the gentleman gave me a look of pure horror, though he kept his hands on the table. What was she summoning this time?

The table settled gently back upon the carpet and did not move again. Something caressed my cheek, leaving cold and damp behind. My heart pounded loud enough to drown the drumming in my distant ears and I knew that I would never be warm again.

The voice that emerged from Madame's lips was one that I dreamt of each night. "Theresa." My name was so faint that I had to strain to hear it.

I trembled in mixture of terrible hope and mortal fear. She had come for me. Here, we might be together once again. But for how long?

A pale cloud formed before us, driving all thoughts from my mind. "Hello, my love." I knew Annabel's voice as I knew my own and the sound of it, even emerging from Madame's mouth, was enough to make me weep for joy.

"Oh, Theresa, how I have missed you." My heart sang, though my ears could detect nothing of love in the way she said the words. I could feel the lady at my side stiffen, and stare at me, but I could not turn to look. Not when the white cloud before me might shift and turn, revealing her beloved features.

"I have missed you, too," I choked out the words with a sob.

"Tell me you love me, Theresa. Tell me how much you have missed me." There was something in the way she said those words that made me draw back: a pleasure, a hunger that was nothing like the laughing girl I remembered.

The gentleman coughed, as if to remind me of his presence. I had forgotten neither him nor the lady at my side nor Madame with her glowing eye, but what if I said nothing and Annabel left? I had spent all my remaining money securing Madame LaFarge's powers: there would be no second chance.

"I will always love you, Annabel. Just as I promised. You are my soul and my heart."

"Then why haven't you joined me, Theresa?" The question made me start and I could feel my fingers tighten on the table. I flinched at the cruel shift in the voice. Annabel sounded cold and contemptuous as I had never heard her before.

But was she not right to despise me? What was there to stop me from following her? I had nothing left, no one to love me or care what I did next.

With utter certainty, I knew what I should do. I pulled my hand from the table to reach for my clutch.

A hiss from Madame told me that she knew that I had broken the circle, but what was that to me? This life could hold no more dangers. Annabel had come for me and I required nothing more from Madame's powers than that.

Now there was only what I might do for myself. Yet, my certainty faded just enough with the sound that I hesitated, my fingers pausing on the edge of the table. "Theresa," Annabel's voice filled the room, her face forming above the table. "Hurry. I long to embrace you again."

I looked up at her pale, pale face hovering above us, her hair floating in a cloud around it. Her eyes were black holes, not the living blue of memory, and I could see Madame's ceiling beyond her, though misted over as if seen through a veil. But her beloved lips pursed in a little smile and I wanted to kiss them again.

I felt a surge of triumph fill me: Annabel had come for me and me alone. I forgot Madame and the others and saw only Annabel herself, smiling as she had in life. How lucky I was!

Whatever else waited for me I could endure because I would be at her side.

I pulled my pistol free from my clutch and the lady seized my wrist in an iron grip. I tried to shake loose as an oath from the gentleman startled us both. He was staring at Madame, his features twisted in anger and terror. I risked a quick glance away from Annabel toward Madame to see what he saw.

Madame's features were slack and expressionless, with the exception of her mechanical eye. That glowed feverishly and far brighter than it had when she entered and we saw it first. It was too bright to gaze at for long, but in the instant that I met it, I saw such things as I hope to never see again, living or dead. Horrors unspeakable and alien glowed in the depths of that eye as if a demon looked upon us from a shell of human flesh.

My companions each responded in their own ways, the gentleman swearing and jumping to his feet, the lady cringing away and covering her face with her hands. Though my flesh crawled, I looked up at Annabel instead, finding my resolve once again. The circle was broken and my hand had been released. I began to raise my pistol to my head.

"Yesss," a voice that was not quite Annabel's emanated from the spirit, crooning in my ears. The hunger in that voice startled me and I looked away from my beloved, meeting Madame's mechanical eye once again. Annabel looked back at me from the gleaming blue light, her hands held out in a supplicating gesture. It seemed to me that I could see chains on her wrists.

Then I knew the truth: Madame was holding her spirit captive. My sweet, loving Annabel was a prisoner in the demon depths of Madame's mechanical eye. And only I could save her.

My heart racing in my chest, I stood and summoned my resolve. The room spun slowly around me and I heard the gentleman give a distant shout. A cold cloud enveloped me, wafting in from beyond this room where our fates were to be decided. "Quick, my love," Annabel's sweet voice murmured in my ear, sounding like her own dear self. "Set me free. Then we can be together again." I could deny her nothing and I acted as my heart told me she wanted me to act.

There was an explosion. Then I must have fainted from the noise, like some missish, green girl, because my senses knew no more for a time. When

I revived, I was alone in the room. My beloved's face no longer floated above me and my heart ached in mortal terror and pain. Had I lost her? Was I wrong about what she wanted me to do?

An acrid smell filled the air, quite unlike the incense or the stench of the river that had filled the room earlier. I sat up, coughing and the room twisted in a blur of carpet and gaslight and table.

I blinked and the world steadied itself, and wondered where the gentleman and the lady had gone. Had I merely imagined them? The thought was too dreadful to dwell upon.

Madame still sat in her chair, but she said nothing. I stood, using the table to pull myself to my feet. Then I could see why Madame was silent: her human eye was a smoking ruin.

I flinched away in horror. Who could have done such a thing?

I looked down at my hand and my pistol held tightly in it. I recoiled, as if that hand did not belong to me. I must be truly mad, then. And I had lost everything that I held dear. What was I to do now?

Some force compelled me to meet Madame's mechanical eye and my Annabel looked back at me. Her hands were no longer supplicating, but her eyes were full of longing. She beckoned me closer to her.

And I dropped the pistol, and ran to Madame's side. I touched the edges of the mechanical eye, trying to imagine that I held my beautiful girl close and could comfort her. Madame's damp, gray flesh caught at my fingers, dragging them away from the eye. From Annabel. I could not bear to see this: I must set her free from this as well.

I looked around, frantic to find the means. There was a knife on a nearby side table and I seized it in my trembling hand. Annabel smiled at me, and that was enough to inspire me.

When Madame's eye was finally my own, I held it in my hand and stroked it gently. "We can be together once again," Annabel's voice crooned. The blue light glowed around her, gentle and welcoming now. I wanted to enter it, to speak with the voices that called me from its depths. "Make it yours, my love. Command the spirits and you may command mine as well."

The notion filled me with a fierce, wild joy: this would replace all that I had lost and we would be together forever. The blue light glowed, and a dozen voices spoke to me at once from its depths. They told me what I must do next.

It was but a matter of resolve, and with that, I have always been blessed with an abundance.

When I was done and able to walk once more, I rolled Madame to the door. I removed her turban and her scarves before I summoned the maid. The glow in my eye compelled her obedience, and together we took Madame to the Thames and left her in its bosom.

Then we returned to the parlor and I commanded the maid to light the fire. "Call me 'Madame LaFarge' now. You may prepare dinner. I am too weary to see any clients tonight, but we will begin again tomorrow." The woman left, trembling.

I placed the turban on my own head and wrapped the scarves around my neck and wrist. Then I spread my hands on the table and listened to the voices of those who had gone before, each one asking me to help them rejoin the land of the living, even if only for a few moments. There would be no trouble commanding them to appear for my clients.

And my love and I would be together always.

From close by, I heard Annabel's laughter, true and joyous as a bell.

Casualties of War

Jeremy Halinen

Only the oldest ghost knew my name. He asked me if he could hold my hand, said he'd been waiting for years. Knock yourself out, I said, not expecting to feel a thing. The others seemed to be hovering somewhere nearby, whispering about my body and whether they could possess it like a demon might. I didn't notice he'd held my hand until he let it go.

The Difference Men

Kat Smalley

It began with Lord Charles Babbage, as these tales are wont to do. Prime Minister Jenkinson's administration – followed by Canning's, then Goderich's – poured money into Lord Babbage's wild idea of the noble sciences, in his words, "within the grasp of a mechanism." It is said that the Iron Duke himself called on Babbage to investigate the progress of the *Difference Engine*. It is known that when the various mathematicians of the age were brought together under the auspices of reforming His Majesty's military, the great innovations of the time were created on Lord Babbage's Engine. In 1848, when the security of the Continent was threatened by insurrection and agitation, the Empire, backed by great steel Behemoths not seen since the days of Genesis, drove through the heart of Nice – Toulouse – Strasbourg – Paris, and crushed the anarchists in their nests.

It was said that When Her Majesty's Armored Cavalry entered the German States and Prussia, it was to protect France from anarchy spilling over the border. Her Majesty's government told the same story when it entered the Hapsburg lands, then Switzerland and to the Italian Peninsula.

With the vastness of Europe under the Empire's watchful eye, the Empire was free to expand its knowledge of the gross and subtle worlds. A great

Laboratory was built in the city of Bath, wherein the Democritean arts were studied at length.

Detective Ambrose O'Sullivan is a tall, lean Irishman in the employ of the Ministry of Internal Security. He is wearing a double-breasted waistcoat, trousers and a bowler hat. When he is certain that no-one is around to watch him, he curses the dust which stains his trouser legs, the unavoidable result of spending any appreciable amount of time in the dusty, dung-strewn streets of the Bombay markets. Detective O'Sullivan does not – as is common for his position – wear his badge, hoping on that half-hearted anonymity to travel unmolested by the throngs of Hindoos and Moslems whose passions against the White man are barely restrained by scores of constables with plasmic guns.

Several days ago, the Chapterhouse in London received a communiqué from Bombay, *viz.* an informant for Her Majesty's government. It seems that a rogue artificer had stolen a goodly sum of radioactive victorium from the Bath Laboratory and fled to India, perhaps solely to construct a Difference Man in a place he thought would be safe.

Detective O'Sullivan takes a small pad of paper from his coat and looks at the notes given to him. The scientist was found dismembered in the most grisly fashion – the members torn from his trunk in the same way a youth might tear the legs from a creeping bug. A day before the Detective made his way to Bombay on the overnight Ventus, the local constables found their informant slaughtered much like the lost scientist – drawn and quartered rather like traitors against the crown in the days of old.

Detective O'Sullivan is inclined to think that the Difference Man that the departed scientist constructed with the stolen victorium is still skulking around the dark crevasses of Bombay. A thought, one that has surfaced before, floats to the forefront of his meditations – he is in India, volunteered by his superiors for a duty which he did not seek. His superiors told him that his previous case would be his last in India, but as he has repeated to himself *ad nauseum,* one always has one's duty to Crown and Empire.

Officially, there have only been a mere handful of Difference Men constructed throughout the Empire, but what is officially said to quell the easily-flustered sensibilities of the hoi polloi, O'Sullivan thinks to himself as he walks through the marketplace, is not always the truth.

There is an old man who labors as a spice-peddler in the marketplace. He is a lean, wiry man, whose noble, Aryan face belies his bitterness towards the duly-appointed agents of the state. Regardless, O'Sullivan knows from personal experience that he regards himself as the warder of this market, as his lineage is of the *Brahmins*, the aristocratic stock of the Hindoos. When the old man sees Detective O'Sullivan coming, he puckers his lips and stares.

"Rakṣaso 'gacchati," the old man spits.

"I know you can speak English, you devilish old crow," Detective O'Sullivan says, "So you can keep your incantations to yourself and speak a civilized language with me."

"You are arrogant as always, Detective Ambrose O'Sulliva," the old man says in a slow, halting voice, his *d*'s and *t*'s rolling against the hard palate of his mouth, as is the habit of the natives of the Raj.

"My arrogance needn't concern you, old crow," O'Sullivan sneers, "What ought to concern you is a Difference Man concealed in this quarter of the town."

"I know of no Difference Men here."

Detective O'Sullivan sighs, reaching into his jacket. He takes from a concealed pocket a curved and polished weapon crafted mostly from titanium. The handle is ebony, inlaid with whirling arabesques of ivory and mother-of-pearl, thus making a peculiar chiaroscuro between the stygian blackness of the wood and the luminescence of the bone and nacre. The old man's eyes grow somewhat wider – he recognizes British guns like that one are capable of evaporating a man's chest from a thousand yards away. Detective O'Sullivan sets it on the rough-hewn wooden table on which the old Brahmin kept sacks of spices – rocks of brown jaggery, withered purplish allspice berries, shillelaghs of clove – and watches the Brahmin's expression as he recognizes the gun.

"I know of *no* Difference Men here," the Brahmin reiterates.

"I am entitled to arrest you if you aid and abet anarchists, old crow," O'Sullivan says.

The Brahmin closes his eyes, inhaling through his nose. O'Sullivan reads a sense of noblesse into the figure and stance of the fakir-*cum*-peddler. A part of his sensibility softens, but the virile aspect of his character keeps those sympathies at bay.

"I do not know where your artifice man is," the Brahmin says, "but I have heard tell that he would be traveling to London. Perhaps he is no longer in Bombay, Detective Ambrose O'Sullivan."

"Pr'haps," Detective O'Sullivan says, "Perhaps you're spinning a wild fable to get me to quit Bombay."

"If I were lying, Detective," the Brahmin says, "you could easily return and make troubles in my marketplace. I cannot lie to you."

Detective O'Sullivan lifts gingerly his gun from the Brahmin's table, replacing it in his coat. Opposite the instrument of death is O'Sullivan's notepad, which the Detective withdraws from a pocket. He opens the cover of the pad and writes something down with a small, worn pencil-nub.

"Do you aver, to the best of your ability, that you believe a Difference Man is headed to London?"

"I do indeed."

"And do you aver, to the best of your ability, that the Difference Man in question will be making his way to London within the fortnight?"

"Today or tomorrow, even," the Brahmin says.

O'Sullivan finishes writing his notes with an unrefined quality to his script, which he has heard referred to as Irish cursive.

"Right, old crow," O'Sullivan says, "I shall look into this matter. Should the evidence corroborate your tale, I shall not return."

The Brahmin puts his hands on the table, watching as Detective O'Sullivan tips his bowler in his direction, turning to depart. Though Detective O'Sullivan is inclined to head back to his office, the notion of a Difference Man set loose on the Metropole of the Empire gives him enough pause that he heads instead to the Ventus station.

Detective O'Sullivan passes through the streets of Bombay, he puts a plan together in his mind. The first Difference Man was named Adam in deference to the memory of the common ancestor of all mankind. The Bath Laboratory brought Adam to be received by Her Majesty at Buckingham Palace. So as not to be in a state of undress before the Queen, Adam was decked out in the colorful robes and turbans of the archaic Jews, in memoriam of the Sons of Israel of which our progenitor Adam's issue would come to belong.

It is said that Minister Disraeli was pleased by the scientists' affectation.

The Queen seemed surprised that a homunculus of gear-work and copper and steel would look so like a man. Yet, when the scientists opened up Adam's breast, the whole of the court gasped at the luminescent spectacle of a cube of anthracite being atomically disassembled for power. Eventually, the scientists managed to construct Difference Men with victorium, though further experiments were later deemed illegal. Adam led the five victorium-fueled Difference Men in a Marxist rebellion in Ireland. The Empire spent five years quelling the insurrection, leaving the Emerald Isle fire-struck and gouged open, soaked in the blood of a million mothers' sons.

O'Sullivan makes his way to the Ventus Grand Central Station. A dozen massive rail lines enter and depart the station faster than the speed of sound, and Detective O'Sullivan watches as hundreds of people filter in and out from the grand building. Those who are exiting are White men and their wives, and many of the various Moslems, Parsees, &c. of India are entering, though they are wearing the civilized clothing of Europe in an effort to conform to the standards of the Empire.

Detective O'Sullivan mounts the stairs, entering the station proper. Massive brickwork pillars abut cyclopean arches which support the marble friezes and the vaunted ceiling of Grand Central. Nestled in the ledges between the arches are statues carved from glistening purple porphyry, which represent the Roman gods most appropriate to the station – swift-footed Mercury, Apollo of wisdom and the sciences, the conquering Jove, Liber, and so on.

It is there that Detective O'Sullivan sees the idol in the flesh.

A boy – for that is what he is, a smooth-chinned Ganymede standing beneath the statue of Jupiter – is peering at a gold pocket-watch, waiting for the two-fifteen to – presumably – King's Cross. Detective O'Sullivan stares despite himself. O'Sullivan's eyes creep across the breadth of the boy's figure, measuring him with all the intimacy of a Savile Row tailor.

The boy's eyes lift from the watch and fix upon O'Sullivan. He does not blink, nor does he avert modestly his gaze. His eyes are blue and blaze almost unnaturally with an inner fire, as if snatched from God's own empyrean. He clicks his watch closed and pushes it back into his pocket, hesitating for a moment as he allowed his form to be made bare by O'Sullivan's unremitting glance. The boy prepares to depart on the Ventus, and tips his small top hat towards Detective O'Sullivan. The Detective does not notice at first the tip of the hat, but instead sees a curl of fair and radiant hair fall from beneath the brim.

Detective O'Sullivan rushes toward the boy, but the throng of travelers impedes his progress – blocks his path as he makes his way to the pillar against which the boy was standing. But when he finally weaves his way through the mass of bodies, the boy is long gone. He heads down the corridor that leads to Platform Five – the platform nearest the pillar. The ticket-taker working at the tube is helping ladies off the Ventus, and he does not seem fazed by the

Detective's approach. The lad is carbuncular, lanky and – it might set a proper father's teeth on edge – seemingly disaffected by his position of responsibility.

"D'yeh have yer ticket, sah?" The ticket-taker asks.

"Young man," Detective O'Sullivan responds, "I am a Detective in the service of Minsec."

Those two clipped syllables – *Minsec* – are enough to cause the carbuncular boy to stiffen involuntarily. His eyes grow wide and he purses his lips so tightly that they become little more than a slit against the blemished white skin of his face.

"Ah – yessah! Please, take a cabin, and Ah'll make th'arrangements. Y'needn't worry 'bout a thing sah, not a thing!"

Detective O'Sullivan nods thankfully, tipping his bowler hat as he climbs the stairs onto the Ventus, his heels tapping – *tink, tink* – against the studded copper. O'Sullivan proceeds to an empty cabin and turns the knob on the inside of the door, marking it as "occupied." The interior of the cabin is luxuriously appointed, with its central table installed with the most modern luminescent tubular lamp, and a circular settee arranged around it, filled with the softest down. The table has several small cavities which, as O'Sullivan knows from memory, are filled with small nuggets of mastic gum.

O'Sullivan sits down on the settee, and his body sinks into the cushioning beneath and behind his form. He reaches beneath his seat and opens a drawer. There are books for the public delectation stored in its cavity. O'Sullivan flips through the titles and takes out one he has not read before – *The Lifted Veil,* a novella by George Eliot, the Madam Evans. He feels the Ventus-car shudder and creak to life like one of the primal juggernauts of the African plains – like a pachyderm crashing against tree branches and knocking them to the earth. He knows well enough the pneumatic science behind the Ventus, unsurprised as the beast comes to life, hurrying like the mythical steeds of the many pantheons, traveling hundreds of leagues in the blink of the proverbial eye.

The door slides open.

"I am afraid I am in no mood," O'Sullivan says, neglecting to look up from the book in his hands, "for tea and biscuits, madam."

"I have not come bearing gifts," a man's soft voice says, "Detective Ambrose O'Sullivan."

One might not notice O'Sullivan's fingers digging into the binding of his book. He throws it on the cushion of the settee and reaches into his coat with all the celerity of a cobra, withdrawing his gun, holding it with both hands as he aims it at the interloper –

But – it is the boy – the Ganymede made flesh. He watches O'Sullivan with a curious glance and collapses his top hat with a click, his form unhurried as he turns to slide closed the cabin door behind him.

"*You* are the Difference Man – my quarry!" O'Sullivan exclaims.

"Perhaps, my good Detective, you have mistaken our roles," the clockwork angel contends, "if you will forgive my impertinence."

The Difference Man walks towards the Detective, his stride calm and measured, like a priest's – O'Sullivan cannot help but envision – as he carries the burning thurible during Mass. O'Sullivan holds up his gun as if it were a warding fetish against earthly evil.

"Stay back, you devil –!" O'Sullivan growls out.

"If you shoot me, Detective, you will pierce my reaction chamber, and all of the passengers in this car will be bathed in radiant particles," the Difference Man blithely says, "they shall die."

"Doubtlessly. But their lives – and mine – are a worthy sacrifice for the security of the Empire," O'Sullivan says.

"Are you so eager to die, Detective?" The Difference Man says.

Though O'Sullivan does not respond, his eyes watch the Difference Man walk towards the settee. The mechanism sets himself upon the cushions, languid, raising a knee and stretching his right arm over the back of his seat, looking for all the world like El Greco's *Sebastian*. O'Sullivan's gun suddenly becomes heavy as an iron weight in his hand. He slides his off-hand beneath the butt of the gun, steadying its deadly aim at the soft angles of his counterpart's torso.

Passengers of the two-fifteen to King's Cross Station, London.

The voice of the attendant – a respectable thing, properly enunciated as one would expect from a woman of quality – rings over the loudspeaker.

"Yet–" the Difference Man says, "I remain unharmed. Perhaps you cling more fervently to life than you admit? Perhaps you are hoping to apprehend me?"

"I am not so foolish," Detective O'Sullivan says, "as to believe that this confrontation shall end in anything but death. What shall I call you, automaton?"

We are preparing to depart. Before we activate the inertial dampeners, please ask your wives to hold your children and restrain any loose items.

"You may call me Kārava."

Thank you for traveling with Ventus Lines.

"A Sanskreet name? You've taken up the cause of the Indian anarchists–" O'Sullivan incredulously asks, "–against your Empire?"

Hail Victory. Hail the Crown.

"It is not my Empire," Kārava says, "Or perhaps I ought to say that I did not choose to be a part of it."

"So you would destroy us–!"

"Thus says the man aiming a gun at me."

Detective O'Sullivan lowers his gun. He lowers his gun by mere degrees, pursing his lips as a disapproving governess might. The Ventus-car creaks against the increasing vacuum in the tube, and O'Sullivan can feel his eardrums pressing against the change in pressure, as if he were diving beneath the surf. The sounds of the Ventus are muffled as if passing through cotton-wool, and the Detective can feel pain from within – something elemental pushing from within his head. With his gun still trained on Kārava, O'Sullivan extends his hand, opening the small indention on the table. He takes a few pieces of the mastic gum and puts them between his molar teeth and the skin of his cheek, chewing the evergreen sap with the slow grinding of a cow chewing the cud.

"I cannot – I *shall* not allow you," Detective O'Sullivan says, "to harm the Empire."

The Ventus-car begins to shake, and pushed to and fro by the forces of inertia, O'Sullivan and Kārava rock against their seats on the settee.

"However, you shall allow the Empire to harm you?" Kārava asks.

"What–?" Detective O'Sullivan says.

"You needn't be afraid, Detective. Not of me," Kārava says.

"I am *not* afraid of *you*," O'Sullivan blusters.

"You are a terrible liar," Kārava says, "Regardless, I say in absolute sincerity that I mean you no harm."

Kārava leans forward, extending his hand in the Detective's direction. His palm is smooth and steady, cupped ever-so-slightly, like the mendicant's hand as he begs for the coin for his daily bread. He does not foist his hand upon the Detective, but rather, offers it as a gift, his form as calm as a convent garden. There is a moment in Detective Ambrose O'Sullivan's breast that is not acceptable for a man of his station. In that thorn-stricken moment, the Detective can visualize perfectly throwing to the settee his gun and taking

49

Kārava by the hand, fleeing from his duties. With both hands in place to steady his gun, the Detective pulls the trigger, firing at Kārava.

Kārava, having determined the trajectory of the shock of plasma beforehand through a complex series of trigonometric calculations, dodges the Detective's shot with relative ease. The burning projectile strikes the settee cushion behind Kārava, which explodes in a storm of fire and superheated gasses. Kārava slides down in his seat and kicks with the precision of an arrow in flight, knocking the gun from Detective O'Sullivan's hands. The gun, fortuitously for Kārava, slides beneath the settee with a clatter, leaving O'Sullivan unarmed. Yet O'Sullivan, trained in the diverse *Artes martiales*, is still a potent foe. He leaps from his seat and comes down upon Kārava. He grabs Kārava by the wrists, pushing him back against the cushions, holding him in place.

"You are under arrest, by order of Her Majesty, the Queen –!" O'Sullivan bellows, his voice rising to a fevered crescendo, his hands clutching Kārava's wrists.

Kārava watches O'Sullivan, whose face has taken on the thunderous cast of one of the High Kings of Ireland, wracked with the most dolorous agonies mortal flesh can produce. As Kārava effortlessly pushes against O'Sullivan's hands, his face retains the same expression as Sebastian – uncorrupted and utterly serene.

Kārava pushes O'Sullivan back into his seat and wraps his fingers – elegant as a latter-day Tchaikovsky's – around O'Sullivan's throat. O'Sullivan writhes against Kārava's intractable hands, croaking – fighting – failing.

"He dhārmika vyādha –" Kārava murmurs.

The moment those words pass the engineered seraph's lips, darkness closes around Detective O'Sullivan's pupils, fixing the image of blond ringlets falling around lapis-blue eyes. O'Sullivan swoons against the settee and he thinks no more.

It is said, when Kārava detonated his victorium reaction chamber in the Palace of Westminster, he cried out:

Hail Victory. Hail the Crown.

Lady V
Levi Hastings

Antique

Arthur Rimbaud (1854 - 1891)
translated by Crispin Fondle

Gracieux fils de Pan! Autour de ton front couronné de fleurettes et de baies tes yeux, des boules précieuses, remuent. Tachées de lies brunes, tes joues se creusent. Tes crocs luisent. Ta poitrine ressemble à une cithare, des tintements circulent dans tes bras blonds. Ton coeur bat dans ce ventre òu dort le double sexe. Promène-toi la nuit, en mouvant doucement cette cuisse, cette seconde cuisse et cette jambe de gauche.

Grace-filled son of Pan! About your brow crowned by blossoms and berries, your eyes, those precious balls, revolve. Stained a wine-brown, your cheeks grow sunken. Your fangs glisten. Your chest resembles a lyre; the chimes circulate down your blond arms. Your heart bats in that belly where the double sex sleeps. Talk your walk at night, moving softly that thigh, this second thigh and that left leg.

The Heart of the Labyrinth

◉

Anthony Rella

"THE MINOTAUR LIVES in Crete."

This pronouncement, cutting through our banter, came from the husky salt-and-pepper dog sitting alone at the far corner of the bar, his shirtsleeves rolled back to expose a white bandage on one arm. He was an infamous man known as Charleston, who had overheard myself and my friends Richard and Bartholomew making sport about the inevitability of "going Greek" that evening.

The "Crete" to which Charleston referred was a temple of manhood and sensual indulgence. Men slogged from every corner of the city to refresh themselves in its hot baths, steam rooms, and dry saunas. A stay at Crete was rumored to cure all manner of ills brought on by hours of hard labor or excessive drink. After a certain hour of the day—as Richard would say, "The hour of my arrival"—those enjoying the revivifying warmth might enhance their pleasure and relaxation by letting his arm fall across his neighbor's lap, or presenting his manhood for others to admire and pay homage. Roughhewn men of the docks and over-dressed dandies would pause in Crete and return home to the loving comforts of wife and child, but men such as I and my friends were not mere vacationers. We were native. Richard was a razor-sharp accountant with a permanent curl of hair hanging over his forehead; and Bartholomew, a rather gruff and heavyset barber who shaved his own pate to the nub.

Every week, my mother and father sent me letters with instructions to greet women with a fine bow and warm smile, that one might look fondly upon me and consent to return with me to the farm to bear grandchildren. I wish for nothing of the kind. I keep myself tidy and impeccable, but few women look to me as a man who would provide them the passion and safety they desire in a home. Even my appearance is of distaste, as a shorter man with olive-toned skin, rumored to be the scandalous inheritance of a grandmother's liaison with an Italian.

I spent my days as a clerk of the police department, reviewing files, fielding inquiries, and ensuring one department has completed its paperwork appropriately and directed it to the appropriate other department. Work had quite exhausted me of late due to a marked increase of inexplicable deaths around the city—men's bodies found in the oddest places, in some cases completely lacking in clothing, injured in ways suggestive of ritual torture. Young, old—men of all kinds. You might imagine the amount of paperwork this caused—I apologize for my callowness, but I was preoccupied with paperwork, particularly when I noticed to my horror that many of the deceased were men I had known as having gone Greek on one or several occasions. The coincidence was so striking that I suspected some underlying unity to these cases, at which the detectives guessed but could not yet discern. I feared to offer my evidence, preferring not to damn all of us.

Here I have wandered into the thicket of particulars and neglected the action. My friends and I recognized Charleston from many awkward encounters witnessed and experienced over the years. He was the kind of man who accepted a moment's eye contact as an invitation to press close with foul sausage breath and attempt to steal a kiss or run his warty fingers along the smooth and sensitive parts of one's body. You might understand the irritation caused by having our private conversation eavesdropped upon by this man.

"We've no interest in your words or attention," I said.

Charleston only slammed his mug of beer and said, "The Minotaur lives in Crete! You must keep yourselves away, particularly from the Labyrinth!"

I neglected to remark upon the most peculiar feature of Crete. Away from the baths and the steam stood a dark portal through which one entered into a series of corridors, twisting and turning, known as the Labyrinth. Of all the architectural complexities of Crete, this one was the most conducive for furtive acts of hedonism.

"Cease with your beer," Richard said. "I fear you have saturated your sanity."

"Damn you all for idiots," Charleston said. With a sharp inhalation of breath, he attempted again. "You must listen. A dangerous beast dwells in the darkest halls of Crete. Men, good men, have wandered in and gone missing."

"Since these men have disappeared in a maze within a place called Crete," Bartholomew said, "You have decided that the myth must have completed itself, with the Minotaur."

"I've seen him. A beast that stalks the darkness, grasping for tender flesh with his claws." Charleston raised his hands into the gesture of claws tearing at the sky.

"I'd say you happened upon a mirror and failed to recognize yourself," Richard laughed.

Finally Charleston soured and acknowledged to his beer that we might, after all deserve, to be found dead in an alleyway. His expression bore weariness and weight, a sorrow that melted my irritation. Here was a man who believed he had gazed into the darkness that consumed his friends, wondering whether or why he was the one to return. These thoughts were bleak, and I attempted to turn my mind to lighter fare. Such thinking, I believed, made people dour and miserable to be around. Sooner would I be accused of "shallowness" than let myself drown in those "depths."

Our mood dulled, my friends and I paid for our drinks and made our way into the frosty autumnal gloom. Crete was a mere fifteen-minute walk from our pub of origin, in the disreputable street known as Sinners' Alley. Here all manner of men and women enjoyed the companionable pleasures of vice. One could get a simple glass of absinthe and sleep quite comfortably in a corner, with only the expectation of an empty pocket come morning. Local businesses hired bruiser-men with silver rings and shiny glass goggles to enhance security. Artists dressed as statues beckoned and danced luridly along the center of the street. Truly it was a place of mirth and freedom, a deep exhalation after a day's propriety and discipline.

The high gray-brick wall featured a simple wooden door adorned by its sign. Inside, translucent glass tubes ran horizontally through the walls, interrupted at junctures by glass orbs that bubbled and steamed. These pipes moved heated water from the furnace below into the baths and steam rooms while warming the building, an ingenious architectural design. The orbs shone with light that apparently passed through filters of rotating color, resulting in a shifting prism.

Bathrobes and bathing towels were provided, further dress discouraged. We opted for the more revealing towels. Simply to shed the shell of daily civilization was a pleasure, to feel the air and the longing gaze of others on one's exposed chest.

The atmosphere of Crete was heady; the spirit of Bacchus fully aroused. Even in the cool pools, I saw men kissing and caressing each other with abandon. A savage virility exuded from me, a desire to claw and consume. Within minutes of relaxing in the pool, Richard and Bartholomew took to petting and pecking each other. We had been friends for three years, seeking intimacy amidst the impersonal morass of urban living. This development, however, was unexpected. I confess I had never imagined any such mutual attraction existing. Whether this suggested a romantic pairing or simply the regrettable impulse of a moment, I felt quite rudely excluded. I admit, I felt jealous.

Mood significantly depressed, I retreated from the pool to the sauna. This provided no satisfaction, as the mean age of that room's inhabitants exceeded my own by a margin I did not appreciate. I wished these men all joy and satisfaction, but I now felt quite irritated and put out. The stresses of the week and this development from Richard and Bartholomew conspired to dispirit me with frustrated desire. I had been primed to hunt, now discouraged by the prey.

Walking the circuit about the baths, I marked the Labyrinth's entrance and recalled our dire prophecy. No wonder one might ascribe something sinister to the place. The darkness promised adventure, risk, and mystery. Exactly what I needed most this night, the concealment of darkness separating the body's pleasure from the eye's discrimination. Through the portal one became divested of those differences of race, class, occupation, age, and appearance.

I looked upon my inner forearm at an old scar, pocked and glaring against the smoothness of skin, from a time that my father deemed it appropriate to lay a heated iron upon me, as punishment for failing to return home from school before nightfall. The smell of whiskey, suffusing him like mist, has often rendered me lightheaded and fearful. I have engaged in amateur study of animal nature and come to question our traditional associations. For it seems, though animals can be cruel, I do not find the depth or breadth of suffering imposed on their own kin as we do to ours. Cats do delight in torturing their prey but may well redeem themselves by offering their killing as sacrifice to a beloved master. I wonder, instead, whether it is our humanity that damages our bestial nature.

I recalled the strange pattern of ruined men littered about the city. Eyes and mouths stretched agape, as though attempting to expel whatever evil was upon them. In addition to the external bruising, tearing about the mouth and anus was not uncommon. The detectives were confounded, with no apparent causality and seemingly no motive. Walking into the darkness of Crete, I fancied for a moment that I could take upon myself the quest for answers. The thought terrified me. Never have I considered myself a person of courage or ambition.

Glass pipes and their orbs continued in parallel strips along one wall, bathing the corridors with shifting-colored light. One could see the outlines of bodies and a flash of flesh. Doors lined the walls, into which one could slide with a partner, or enter alone and peer through a hole that opened into the neighboring cell. Anonymity made more anonymous, sexuality narrowed until the encounter was entirely between a cock and a set of lips. The thrill of this is hard to describe. One could imagine fellating a god who walked among men, or offering devotion to the Lord of Earthly Delights and receiving his boon in turn.

An urgency in my heart goaded me forward, as though I could find pleasure if only I walked more deeply into the Labyrinth. Within minutes I reached a strange juncture. The glass orbs abruptly stopped at another portal, a gateway marked with some inscription that was impossible to read with the available light. One man lingered on the lit side of the gate and reached forward, clutching my towel to pull me close. The fur of his beard felt warm against my cheek as his lips and breath tickled my ear.

"Came to spend a little time with me?" Incredibly, I knew the answer was no. Gently taking his hands and bringing them down to his sides, I stepped away.

"I wish it were so, but I seem to be in a restless mood. All I want for now is to walk."

"Then you'd best go no further. Turn back to finish your walk."

"Is it so dangerous? Do you believe this story of the Minotaur?"

The man's voice had a tremulous quality. "Last week I was with a friend, Baxter, who ventured back there. I waited more than a few hours but never saw him again. I assumed I had missed him, but later heard rumors that he ran from this place, naked and terrified, in the hours of early morning after I left."

My heart beat ferociously as I recalled the case file of one man identified by the name of Baxter. I inquired about the particulars of the man, a stocky baldheaded gent with a great long beard.

"Yes, have you seen him?"

The note of hope itself touched my heart, and I felt the urge to fold the man in my arms and give him whatever comfort I could. I had seen Baxter, laid out in the autopsy room. The forensic detective had requested reports of prior victims for comparison's sake. Upon the autopsy bed, the curtain of Baxter's chest had been parted to reveal its contents. He lay like a dissected specimen. Typically I avert my eyes from such sights but happened to notice the greenness of the man's still wide-open eyes. That glimpse evoked for me who Baxter had been in life. I could remember instances of seeing him at the pubs or walking in Crete. His body was thick and heavy, but moving with a lightness that spoke of the ferocity of his being. Baxter was a man who was quick to light up in smile and laughter. His caresses, even uninvited, rarely evoked irritation or disgust, for he so generously offered his admiration for beauty without any apparent need for appreciation in return. The juxtaposition of these memories with the vision of him exposed upon the table seemed wrong, as though I disrespected one by adding the other.

"I know of him," I admitted. "Some people I know are also curious about what happened to him."

"Once or twice he has vanished like this. I found him later in tears after a torrid affair. I cannot explain why, but I fear the worst has happened. I stand here hoping that he might wander out and smile as though all were well."

Sweating, I felt as though I should know what to say but simply wanted to escape. I made a movement to continue, but the man stepped forward. "Please consider," he said. "Whatever you seek, you could find here." I touched his chest and pressed a delicate kiss on his cheek. I fancied that we could become lovers if I remained. Sentimental, I understand, not even knowing his name. Whatever might have begun would have already been compromised by my failure at the door. An inner call bade me to continue, and I obeyed.

The corridor was utterly dark. I walked slowly, testing the ground with my toes, my feet whispering across the floor. Right-angle turns of the Labyrinth softened into gentle curves, unbroken by doors into privacy chambers. Rather the walls narrowed and smoothed like rock worn by the ocean. No one else seemed to have ventured this far. I wondered whether this was an original feature of Crete or an extant tunnel from previous constructions, leading to the city's underworld. I must be descending, I thought, else I could not fathom how these tunnels fit within the building as I had known it.

My rumination abruptly ceased. Every sense dilated. Ahead I noticed a change in the darkness. A low glow, not yet a light. Then the sound came.

Walking through the Labyrinth, one grew accustomed to love-sounds emanating from the corridors, mingled as they often were with the snores of those who had worked too long and drunk too heartily. The sound I heard now was as similar to those grunts and moans as the dog is to the wolf. Shrieks and guttural sounds heralded ferocious lovemaking or some kind of torture, returning to silence almost as quickly as they had emerged.

Though alarmed, I did not then feel at threat. Bartholomew had shared with me tales of his encounters with men who became aroused by causing pain, and I suspected this to be the cause. Perhaps, I reasoned, only those interested in the darkest hues of sensuality dared to venture this far into the heart of Crete. So I continued.

The glow ahead grew into flickering warm orange and soon I came upon a painting flanked by two open-flame oil braziers. A rather strange, medieval decoration. The piece depicted the copulation of a snow-white bull and a Rubenesque woman concealed within the cage of a wooden cow, presenting herself. Some lines of verse had been written beneath the painting:

To lay with beasts, Reason unheeded:
Such Monstrous things thereby are breeded.

I cringed at the author's torturous shaping of these lines to suit his moralistic purpose. Not ten feet away was a portrait of the Minotaur itself, posing with ferocious eyes and imposing musculature, bearing a sovereign staff in one hand and extending the other, open-palmed, toward the viewer. Its name was given, Asterion, the stellar beast. Supernatural force given human reason and terrible form. Was this, then, the Minotaur of which I had heard such dire portents? I began to laugh. I could easily imagine a terrified man rounding the corner and coming upon these paintings, frightening himself into frenzy. Had my imagination seized upon unrelated crimes and begun to formulate a fantastic story?

My laughter quieted with the sudden chill of skin. As before, something outside awareness alerted me to danger. Without the heating tubes, the Labyrinth was like a winter prison, and I with only a towel was beginning to shiver. My feet had grown cold and numb upon the stone floor. My good sense finally took hold, and I decided to return to the baths of Crete and inquire about these paintings.

My heartbeat sharply accelerated, however, turning back. Two floating orbs in the corridor reflected back the torchlight, moving toward me. A large animal walking on two feet became illuminated. The orbs were its eyes, half the size of a man's fist, dull and unblinking. Two scaly horns protruded from either side of its head. For a moment I was immobilized, attempting to comprehend the reality of what approached. Finally, horror overtook me and I simply turned to sprint deeper into the Labyrinth.

After a few curves, I was again in darkness. I paused to gather my breath and thoughts, beating heart seeming to drown out all other sound. The strangeness of the situation must have agitated my imagination, I thought. Perhaps I perceived horror where there was not. Presently I heard the beast's scraping footfalls draw near. I disregarded reason and ran forward.

Before long, the chill receded. Rounding a corner, I collided with a wall of hot air as I entered the heart of the Labyrinth. This was a cavernous room, illuminated by a blazing coal furnace. This oven was joined by an elaborate system of gears, chains, and pipes to a cistern of water, from which glass tubes extended into the ceiling. Here lay the engine and source of Crete's ingenious water system. This hellish laboratory gave potency to the steam and soothing water in which the men above delighted. A pile of coal to my right lay beneath an open ceiling chute. Deliveries of coal must have been shunted into a hole outside of Crete, finding its destination here. To my left lay a large mattress where something must have slept, perhaps the laborer who fed the machine. What laborer could tolerate this heat? I had not long to wonder before turning to face the beast.

As the creature moved about the room, its face seemed to shift and contort. When I thought I understood its appearance and nature, my view revealed something new and concealed the rest. Was this beast or devil, deformed human or mutation? The beast's body was indeed humanoid, muscles rippling from hours of labor feeding the furnace. It walked with bold, lumbering gait, a cocky young sailor's swagger. The slow walk that conveys the strength of the man, the certainty that he could have you. The creature's jaw jutted forth and nose flared and bent upward such that the contents of nostrils were apparent. What disgusted and fascinated most were what might have been human ears grown scaly and bony, contorted and stretched into what I had believed were horns. Swollen goiters bulged in its neck like secondary heads, as though other men within pressed out for liberation. With the light and heat, the chaos of the moment, I cannot justify which impressions were accurate and which were inflamed. The beast was wholly nude, cock slapping gently against its left thigh, a member that could split apart an unprepared man.

Here, I believed, was the true Minotaur, the origin of myth and rumor. Could it have left the confines of its native Greece and come to another Labyrinth, where it might lay in wait for prey? My body felt numb and static, like the bird preparing for the cat's final blow. The Minotaur came so near that its sour breath caressed my cheek. In the dark orbs of its eyes, I saw myself bare of protection and self-deceit, pathetic and vulnerable and utterly, undeniably mortal. I would not have the chance to grow ungraciously old, to wrest myself from my decades-long prison of fearfulness and dare to make something of my life. Now the Minotaur would consume my soul and send my body screaming into the world, to be found cold and stiff in some disgusting alleyway, zipped into a bag, cut apart by surgeons, and scrutinized by forensic specialists with detached curiosity. None would remember my name.

The beast's attention was caught by the scar upon my inner arm. With callused hands it took my arm to gaze upon the iron's pattern.

"You have known hurt." The voice grumbled from its very pit, roared like the furnace. "How was this done?"

"Punishment. From my father," I said simply.

The beast let my arm drop. "What will you miss most of the life you have lost?"

"Nothing," I stuttered. "Nothing to miss. I made nothing of my life."

"What has oppressed you?"

"This shadow cast over my heart," I said. "I've always lived in the cold."

"You fear the heat, to be burned again." The Minotaur grabbed both of my shoulders and pulled me toward the great furnace. Flame roiled behind iron teeth. Upon the furnace was a metal sigil, a circle with horns, glowing orange. "If you were to be free, would you live the life you've been given?"

Not knowing what I was being asked, I said yes. The Minotaur grabbed my unscarred left arm and laid it upon the searing-hot sigil. That was my last memory.

I awoke in a cramped, dark cell. A coffin, I thought, or a morgue closet. Around me, I could hear the familiar sounds of conversation, lovemaking, and snoring. My mouth was dry and my head and arm fairly ached with pain. Feeling along the wall, I found the door's latch and discovered I had been returned to the outer edges of Crete's Labyrinth. My heart welcomed the light of those glass orbs, though the sight now evoked the horror of knowing what labored beneath us to maintain this pleasure-dome.

Exiting the Labyrinth, I found the baths and saunas largely empty. The time must have been near dawn, when the only men left were those with nowhere better to be. Bartholomew and Richard were nowhere to be found, no doubt departed without concern for my well-being. Shocked and concerned gazes told me all I needed to know of my appearance. Pain from the charred flesh of my inner arm was difficult to bear. The sigil of Taurus would no doubt be with me for life.

Taking my clothes, I found the one man left on staff and was unsurprised to find he claimed no knowledge of the Minotaur, though I noted he did not seem startled by the state of my arm. I made my way to the hospital, where the staff was alarmed by the severity of my injury and my inability to account for its cause. Their condescending remarks suggested I had inflicted it upon myself from some perversion. I sharply urged them to attend to their work.

We Greeks were condemned to diaspora within a week, as Crete shut its doors. Another man had been found dead the morning after my encounter with Asterion, this one a notable Alderman whose murder could not be obscured by police investigation. He had been seen entering Sinners' Alley, and I made certain to offer hints and suggestions to bring the detectives' investigation into sharper focus. All was in vain, however, as Crete had been vacated in earnest. A warrant to search the property uncovered nothing of use. Concrete sealed the gateway to the deeper layers of the Labyrinth.

A month after my encounter, I was again in the pub where Charleston had made prophecy about the Minotaur. He was there, engaging in conversation with three gentlemen who treated him with reverence and care. Having no companions, I arranged myself to sit beside him, where I could overhear the prophet offering words of quiet wisdom and guidance in addition to his usual salacious overtures. He spoke with a generosity of spirit that was given back in turn by his disciples. As the men departed for their own adventures, Charleston turned his head slightly toward me, perusing me with a glance. I could not gather whether he recalled me. An instinct caused me to unbutton my left cuff and draw back the sleeve to reveal the still red and sore sigil. Silently, Charleston rolled up his own sleeve, revealing the ridges and curls of his matching brand.

"You spoke the truth," I offered. "We were fools to ignore you."

"What else could you have thought?" Charleston sighed. "I am sorry you encountered the beast, but thankful that you are alive."

"I do not understand why."

"Neither do I. Good men lost their lives, but you and I sit here, marked, as though he claimed us."

"To what end?"

Charleston ordered a shot of whiskey for each of us. The scent stirred my familiar nausea, beneath which I sensed resolve, and I drank it all. "I suspect—I wonder whether the Minotaur sees in us something of himself," Charleston continued. My face must have become transparent, for he laughed at my disbelief. "An awful thought, I know. I can only guess as to why I was spared, or marked. What I do know now is that, should he come to seek me again, I want to be ready for death. I want my life to have mattered."

We continued our conversation for an hour before I felt the need to excuse myself. Charleston and I did not part as friends, but with a sense of familiarity that convinced me I would speak with him again. Whiskey dulled the subtle ache of the brand, but the wet, chill air plucked the heat from my body. Outside, the streets were bustling and filled with people going about their lives, eyes narrowed against the wind.

Minotaur
Levi Hastings

Psychopomp

◉

Lydia Swartz

NEVER TRY TO mount and ride a dead horse, who is as capable of speech in the afterlife as you are. Even if you do not mind being cussed out by a dead horse, you should know it annoys Miss Patty, who is after all the psychopomp and makes all the decisions. Do you want to spend your next lifetimes as, say, a cockroach or a continuously pregnant possum?

After watching for a long time, I believe the dead who pester Miss Patty for work to do are the ones doomed to be fitted for a new mortal suit without visiting any of the more sublime, Renaissance-ceiling realms. They do not get where they are, these dead. They annoy Patty the most. If you want to cry for the dead, cry for the ones who waste their afterlife.

If we were not too terrified to reason at first, certain things would be obvious. For instance, whales and octopi swim among us. Bears and crows can talk. We all comprehend each other. Language does not require voices or words. If we thought it through, we might conclude this is not simply human bullshit at a different altitude. But at first we are too terrified to think at all.

Dead rich people are denied the luxuries of the afterlife. They are issued one pair each of baggy cotton boxers and the pot belly to go with it. Among the dead, only the rich cannot understand or speak to dead fish, birds, reptiles, insects, mammals, and humans. (The insects and fish are the most interesting.) The dead rich soon give up trying to get anyone's attention. They stand alone, awkwardly. Nobody can bear to look at them.

The newly dead try to cry. They have no tears. They have no voices. But they think they are supposed to grieve. They make an effort to yearn for those they left lifeside. They hope for attention, comfort, relief — or escape from death, much as they once dreamed of release from the suffering of life. Eventually, even the most expert at self-pity realize that crying binds them to their bodies, which are their biggest lie now.

I would have guessed much sooner that I am dead, but I was fooled by Miss Patty. Who expects a 4-foot-tall, rosy-cheeked, pigtailed psychopomp with a smoke-graveled voice?

Given the relentless efficiency of afterlife communication, I know how much Miss Patty detests me. I cannot blame her. Only to me, you see, is she the foul-mouthed and chain-smoking Miss Patty, the height-challenged, multimillenial cheerleader. I follow her around with big love in my nonexistent heart. A little dignity, please, Miss Patty barks at me as Anubis. But then she goes back to being a cute chain smoker.

Is there romance after death? I boldly ask Miss Patty. Glamorously grumpy, she turns and calls me a name: SUCCUBUS. Then she whirls around again so fast that if her blonde pigtails existed they would strike my cheek, if my cheek existed. I am more smitten than ever. If only I could stop raping her with my ideas. If only I could finish dying and leave her in peace. It is appalling.

The dead who did not believe in an afterlife are the most attached to the carapaces they left to rot lifeside. They look for combs to groom their hair that they don't have. They modestly cover parts no one cares to rape, even if we were able. They are afraid to catch something from the formerly contagious. They don't get it. So we fuck with their heads. We cough on them. We leer at them. We do this as a kindness. It teaches them, or it should.

The story about the tunnel with the light at the end is the second funniest joke among the dead. The third funniest joke is the story where your mentors from lifeside greet your death flight, holding up cards with your name in their dead hands and smiling dead smiles. That is a knee slapper, if we had knees.

The dead can dance. This is not about what you might have listened to in the 1990s while wearing too much black eyeliner. This is a fact: The dead dance. The dead dance without bodies, which means all moves are possible. Dead horses, platypuses, octopi, earthworms, stingrays, slow lorises, brown recluses — everything can dance in the afterlife. You lifesiders experience this as wind.

The pre-dead already think I am talking about heaven or hell or whatever your lifeside mythology calls it. You think we are ghosts or souls. Nope. We have no reason to haunt the lifeside. We have no legacy. We have no agenda. There is no such thing as regret for life or afterlife. We blame no one. We praise no one. We do not need gods as the pre-dead do. For however long we must be, we are; until we learn how to not be.

Undead zombies and immortal blood-drinking vampires are lies made up by the ignorant pre-dead. None of the dead are interested in spending eternity lifeside. Being dead frees us from wanting (unless you are crap at being dead, like me). The dead have no interest in settling scores, achieving closure, getting laid, drinking blood, eating brains, or fighting wolves. True, the newly dead do briefly go through that awkward phase where they try to fuck. Embarrassing for them. Hilarious for us.

We dead hang onto our stories. They clothe us in lies. As persons, we had to have stories to stay alive, but here we must lose them to learn not to. Soon or never, we let go of our stories. We disappear to those still glued here by lies. What really happens is that we go free. Actually, I do not know what happens next. I am still wearing my lies. In fact, I am still collecting lies.

The luckiest dead are the artists. You cannot make anything here except art. The bored dead envy the artists. Artists are the only busy dead.

Boredom is the destroyer. There is no scuffling to survive here; we already failed at that. We do not eat or shit. We do not mate or experience heartbreak. We have no elections nor do we gamble; there is nothing to win. No one goes to school or plays board games or works or exercises.

You cannot sleep when you are dead. It is not insomnia. There is simply no need for it. When the newly dead lie down and shut their eyes, it is the fourth funniest joke in the afterlife. I forgot to tell you that when the newly dead try to fuck, that is the first funniest joke in the afterlife.

I know stories bind the dead to the lie of our bodies. Although I have rid myself of my story or I have forgotten it or else I never had a story, I am still bound. If I were not a story succubus I would be free. But I am addicted. The dead are irresistibly ripe with story. I ask and stories drop into my hand easily. I must harvest. I must. I swallow story like a dumpster. I am a story landfill. Story is my service, my forbidden career in the land of the idle dead.

Right after the newly dead finish their "why me" drama is the best time to harvest story from them. The story is always about how they died. You'd expect this to be short — stroked out in childbirth; blown up in combat; stepped off curb while texting; swallowed shotgun; chemo failed; etc. The end. But the tails are long on these stories. There is where and how and who to these stories. I have the appetite for all of it.

I carry the stories of all the dead in my deceptively flat belly that I don't have. I am sick with gorging on story. If I had a story of my own, it long ago prolapsed under the burden of other stories. Everyone gives stories but no one takes any. With no one to take them, the stories are lost. I am lost. Sometimes I blubber like the most craven of the newly dead.

I am crap at being dead. Even the mute rich, with their standard issue baggy boxers and pot bellies, are better at letting go and moving on. I insist on performing my job, harvesting stories, which is not my job. The dead do not have jobs. Also, the dead do not have stories, just lies they cling to because they have not learned any better. Do you see what I mean? I am crap at this.

I try and I try to let go. Trying to let go is of course the opposite of letting go. I keep doing it wrong. Such as being a story succubus, which is a job, which is wrong. Such as, I am passionately in love with my psychopomp. Wrong. Also, I wallow in despair: so wrong. I despair about despair: meta-wrong. Then why not lean into wrongness? What if I decide to be a libertine among the dead? Wrong is right. I celebrate my wrongness. I let go into my rich, sensual wrongness.

Miss Patty refuses to tell me anything about being a story succubus. Is this even a thing, I ask, or am I just another deluded hobbyist deadster who lacks the courage to quit my day job? I can remember all the stories I have harvested. I cannot remember my own story from lifeside. Was I originally a person? Patty will not answer me. In fact, now when I come at her with the question, she turns Anubis and snarls and sinks her sharp, yellow, nonexistent teeth into my tender, bloody, absent forearm. O Patty. How I love you. How I wish that hurt.

A dead libertine, a jolly afterlife criminal, I yield to my most feral and ridiculous impulse. I sashay up to Miss Patty and I ask for her story. Are you dead? I inquire. How did you become a psychopomp? What were you before you became a psychopomp? Which former person was your favorite client? What do psychopomps do for fun? Is there even a number for how old you are? I do not expect answers. I only wish to horrify Miss Patty by asking.

Usually when Miss Patty scorns me, I see a wee chain-smoker with blonde pigtails flouncing away. But sometimes she gets so angry she manifests as Anubis, then Elegba, then Hermes, then Azrael, then a valkyrie, then Charon, then Shinigami, then the archangel Michael, then Mercury, then Jizo, then Gabriel, then the Grim Reaper.

O rage. O ancient power of transformation. My nonexistent genitals plump for the power to end everything and for the cycle that never ends. I want to touch this power in its manifold forms. Drink it, dance to it. Drown in it. Miss Patty knows this and hates me. Now that you know it, you hate me too. I do not care.

Miss Patty, I love you forever. I think we both know what that means.

The Resurrection Spell

Oscar McNary

Jesus' sweat spiced John's tongue.
While they slept, soldiers splintered
the door and pried the men apart.
Romans pinned Jesus to wooden beams,
an insect in a gradeschool god's collection.
Night after night in John's eyelid cinema,
he watched his lover suffocate in the sun.
John sharpened stories to cut himself out
of the grief net. In wish vision, he unhinged
the talons of the tomb.

I am the apostle beneath an asphalt cross.
This is my gospel.
I disinterred a resurrection ritual: the earth
is a hungry god. No one escapes
her without a trade, a heartbeat peak for a flatline.
I drank a swarm into my belly. I stung
an engine roaring down the sidewalk.
I chose a lamb without spot.
As the groundmouth swallowed the slaughter,
I choked my beloved out of its throat.
My skin warmed the grave out of him.
His eyes were faulty flashlights,
flickering, while he lasted.
The saints warned the guilt of the kill will lay eggs
in your flesh and eat you from the inside. Your silence
will cordon wasteland between living and awakened.
He will fade quickly. His tethered atoms yearn
to feed a hungry god.

Carmilla
M.S. Corley

Moon Goddess
Imani Sims

Body glove
                    Dream catcher

She is creature winged
ash and talon beak
Owl,   draped in gown
of crushed moths,

all eyes.   Night terror
with golden eyes,
                    venom dripping
from her fangs,
She is the one sending
suspended hearts into arrest,

Turns them stone with eyelash
                    gaze.

Earthen Medusa
commanding tide.

Study in Blue, Green and Gold

✵

John Coulthart

FELICIEN WAS THE only rider in the tram that took him to the Salvage district. The vehicle laboured up the incline of Smaragdine-way with its pantagraph cracking in the humid air, rattling through the layers of mist as though emerging from a vapourous sea. Salvage-hill seemed from its summit to be cut off from the city by the ocean of fog, an island of industry palisaded by solitary factory chimneys and reefs of furnace towers. The Black Sun blazed from a clear night sky, searing the city with inverted light. Now that his journeys to Salvage-street were a regular occurrence, Felicien always waited for the moment when the tram crested the hill and Line Seven came into view. On this warm, fume-saturated evening the railway viaduct was a causeway that spanned a city-wide flood of opaque mist, a strange sight even in these stranger days, as though the mantle of cloud had been cut from its moorings and fallen to the earth. The scale of the viaduct beguiled him still, so unlike the mean and timid constructions of the Arnheim Quarter. But the company there beguiled him the more, as did the freedom that company embodied. The boys of Salvage-street reminded him of the Young Savages but without the insouciance and limited vision which had made him tire of his former friends; he thought of Audrey and the others as his real family.

An hour later he was looking down from the soot-blackened wall of the viaduct into the sea of earth-bound clouds. Audrey and his friends had passed around the stelons before they climbed the flights of stairs up to the railway tracks. The portion Felicien swallowed was making its presence known in the buzzing he felt at the back of his head and the weightlessness of his limbs. 'Flying' they called it, and the view over the Salvage district justified the label. But with the levees of his senses yielding to the pressures of a psychotropic flood he felt more like a swimmer: the lights in the streets below were the lamps of a fabulous aquarian city, a submerged world where sleek and lustrous cars glided through the channels of amorphous streets.

—emerald fish with jewelled eyes—

The boys and girls of Salvage-street stood or sat on the rails and sleepers of a disused line, smoking lizard-dust in little clay pipes and drinking bottles of palinka someone had stolen from a warehouse the day before. Torchlights pierced the clouds of steam the enormous trains trailed through the night. Trixie Blade the drag-boy was there, schoolgirl-clad in white shirt, white socks and a short blue skirt with a feather boa. She carried her skenes in a small shoulder-bag of bright blue leather, and welcomed Felicien with a kiss that left a lipstick imprint on his cheek. Alcina and Iris sat entwined, shouting mockery at Audrey while he wandered, inept impresario, among the scattered friends, coaxing them into a party mood. Luca pulled him onto the crate where he was sitting then they spent a few inebriated minutes trying to light a fire. Their butterfly jackets smeared peacock strokes of green and gold through swathes of night while the locomotives blasted the reveries with light and steam and violent noise, thundering out of the dark like iron buildings impelled at speed on their shining paths. The mighty expresses thrilled Felicien with their proximity and their power, the double-decked carriages that shuddered the viaduct in their passing, trailing gales of anthracited air.

—drawn through a tunnel of polychrome panes where the engines proliferate and windows flare with topaz fire, they ripple in layer upon layer of manifold phantom procession—

After a while some of the boys undressed and played acrobat games on the empty rails, impersonating tightrope walkers while they balanced in the torchlight beams. Felicien was more than usually excited watching them discard their clothing, and he wondered whether Audrey had put anything in their drinks; Luca said something earlier about castaphrenic dust. He watched Alcina kissing Iris with her hand thrust into her partner's velvet pants; behind them the naked boys tugged playfully at their erections. Luca beckoned Felicien over and he helped the pair they called the Torso Twins out of their leather harnesses. The tall one named Tetu had no arms, and showed his agility by taking a knife in his mouth, tossing it into the air then catching the handle in his teeth. His lover, Tatu, was limbless from the waist down; he flipped his body over his head to walk the rusted rail on his hands. His genitals had been removed a month before, and the scar between the stumps of his legs was still a vivid crimson stain. They timed their acrobatics to the music crackling from Audrey's glowing wireless, the one he kept tuned to Radio Kaleidoscope. When Hallucination Guillotine blasted out the chords of "Coelacanths In Silver" he turned the volume dial until the old machine rattled with noise.

The stelons were melting the edges of the world. Felicien leaned against the viaduct parapet watching Trixie Blade juggle her skenes. The three blades became an interlaced blur of scattered light and reflected mist that forged a column of razor steel in the smoky air. A boy sitting near Alcina was more concerned with Felicien than with the acrobatics. Dark, well-tended hair with a fringe swept over darker eyes. He and Felicien commenced a game of glance and counter-glance until the boy rose and wandered over. His chest was bare under a blue velvet waistcoat; a choker of shells embraced his throat.

—the Dreamcat sits on the blanketing mist, watching the trains in their furious passing, and the gilded cats which comprise its substance shimmer and blink in jewelled unison, multifoliate idol on the seething fume—

'Are you real?'

'I hope so,' Felicen said. 'Are you?'

'I hope so too—for both of us.' The boy laughed. 'It's hard to tell once these stones start working. I'm still not used to them.'

'I'm getting used to them. Well . . . I think I am. Then they go and make everything different again.' He was watching the Cat while he spoke, awestruck by its presence half a mile away, enormously perched on the mist like a sculpture of filigreed metal. It was larger than he remembered; he wondered whether the others could see it.

'I'm Philip, by the way.'

'I'm Felicien.'

'That's a lovely name. You're not from the Angles, are you?'

Felicien laughed. 'No. From the Arnheim Quarter. About as far from the Angles as you can get.'

—the Agkistrodon uncoils itself from the night, trailing amethyst loops across the vapour, hissing its pictograms into a breeze which pulls them to ribbons of coloured smoke—

'I don't know, there's worse places. I like your beads.' The boy reached out to the black stones at Felicien's throat. The sudden touch of warm flesh against his skin was a dizzying thrill. His penis, swollen already at the sight of the naked boys, pushed hard against the fabric of his trouser leg.

—*the Cat is aroused and with languid grace pads silently over the the sea of cloud, watching him with splendent eyes—*

'I've not seen ones like yours before.'

'These? They're shells. A friend in the Desert bought them for me.'

'Oh, I always wanted to go down there. But I never had the money for the train. I suppose I could now I'm working.'

'What do you do?'

'Apprentice to an alchemist. No, it's not as interesting as it sounds. In fact I don't enjoy it any more, he scares me.'

'I know what you mean. I've serviced a couple of them.'

'Serviced?'

'In the molly-house. Where I work.'

'Oh. That's . . .'

'Not as interesting as it sounds!' They both laughed. 'What's he like then, your alchemist?'

Felicien shrugged. 'I try not to think about him. He doesn't do any magic tricks, though.' He nodded to Luca who was muttering one of the hexes he knew, using a pointing bone to levitate small stones at his feet.

Philip looked over the parapet at the dim vehicle lights moving through the fog on Carsten-way. 'This mist is a strange business. I suppose it's only to be expected these days. I saw something stranger when I was down in the Desert—a huge pillar in the middle of nowhere. Must have been about a mile high.'

Felicien was staring at a trail of small blue flowers which the torchlight had revealed, fragile cups of azure amid the cinder and grime. So very blue there in the dark.

'What is it?'

'What? Oh, nothing.'

—*the Cat climbs the viaduct rampart and pulls itself onto the tracks with unhurried motion, arranging its essence to study him with a patient regard, eyes twin stones of polished tourmaline whose prism deeps ensnare the light—it pays no heed to trains which pass nor to a locomotive at its imminent approach, not even the spears of lamps which pierce its glittering form and flare and grow until train and feline phantasm meet—*

—explosion!—

—the train thunders by in a panelled blur of light and stained-glass lustre and the Cat is a bursting, chiming cloud of a billion tiny gilded replicas, disintegrated shivering feline fragments which race and fly in the violated air then re-corporate swiftly to larger forms—constellated cats that sparkledance and gather themselves from disarray to build again a roiling corpus of greater selves, and those selves repeat each resurrection on and on until the whole of their singular being is restored—

While Philip turned his dilated pupils to the light and noise of the passing train, Felicien stole a glance at his body: the naked chest, the strained fabric wrapping the boy's slender thigh, the erection there outlined. Then Philip was returning his gaze, and he was indrawn by the black wells of those eyes, so dark they seemed, all dark and aglitter with tiny points of light in a face that thrilled him with its delicate features, everything around them—stones and trains and air and night—raptured with transcendent moment.

'Someone gave you a kiss.'

Philip smiled, and ran the tip of a finger over the lipstick on Felicien's cheek.

—and the finger attended by myriad foliations in a fading trail—

The lightest touch yet it summoned a delirium, a swimming of senses already in turmoil, and with it came that moment of absolute conviction when he knew that sex was inevitable.

'I like kisses,' he whispered, breathless and dazzled. A nimbus of neon moiré blazed about the body of the boy. He gently grasped the perfect head and put his tongue inside the mouth, and while they kissed he ran his hands on the naked chest, the soft muscles there—so warm and tender!—and stroked the skin within the velvet, forcing with his fingers a drool of fluid from the column of cotton-clad flesh which pressed against his groin.

They parted for a moment and looked at each other and laughed.

'Oh . . .' Felicien said, 'I feel . . .'

'So do I!'

Like nothing he'd known before. They kissed again, and he melted in a bliss of bodily warmth. Somewhere in the distance the other boys whistled and applauded. His cares of the previous days had vanished like the shreds of locomotive steam.

—the Agkistrodon raises its substance between the tracks and oil-slick stones as though summoned by music from the rattling radio—phallic amethyst coiled high above them, mysterious and graceful, silent adherent to its golden accomplice—

When the Black Sun became too much to bear they took their pipes and bottles and the blaring wireless a short way down the track to an abandoned carriage the boys had discovered a year before. The seats had been stripped out, new locks fitted to the doors, and all of the windows secured. The floor was layered with old mattresses and heaps of cushions. Rugs decorated the walls and the ceiling was covered with mirrors and sheets of polished tin. Audrey called it 'The Salvage Rumpus Room'.

Felicien led Philip by the hand up the carriage steps. Once inside they fell on the nearest quilted pile.

—the spectral beasts enter through the wall, discorporated to mineral fragments and slowly spiralling gilded swarf which retains an animate intelligence while it meanders in incense-tinted air—serpent shards leak symbol smoke while the scintillated feline teases the space with a palindrome murmur—

'You two are eager,' Audrey said, and he laughed while he lighted candles to scent the gloom. The others filed in but Felicien was too preoccupied to notice. He opened Philip's trousers then fell upon the unveiled penis that slapped against a trail of hair. Transformed by rapture to a sacred object, the flushed icon of masculine ecstasy demanded veneration, so he put his lips to the burning head and drew forth its stream of nectar, adrift in an orbit of visions like those from his Young Savage nights.

—a great copper sphere whose corroded surface ruptures in riverine cracks that reveal a chaos of interlaced machinery—

Audrey's stelons inspired the company to other venerations, for the bodies of their partners or for themselves. Those still clothed were soon disrobed, and the soft wireless music was accompanied by softer gasps and moans while limbs entwined in a perfumed chiaroscuro of amber light.

—as it might be some Hermeneutic marvel from the age of the Aethyromantic Engineers—and more—a mechanistic planetoid suspended in an abyss where the stars are changed—

Felicien shook off his remaining garments then lay down again facing Philip's waist. While they lost themselves in each other a voice intoned from the sighing shadows: Audrey was reading by the light of a candle from his book of poems.

Come boys of gold with angel wings unfurled,
Loosed from your aethyrs, here your pleasures seek,
Come light the darkest corners of our world,
We crave your touch and long to hear you speak.

—movement lights the darkened fractures and phallic butterflies fly forth, carapaced marvels in quicksilver gleaming with wings of shimmering silk—and more—

So speak to me and gift me with your fire
Of flesh that smoulders with a rare delight,
Lave me with golden milk of your desire,
And spend your lust across the violet night.

—they flicker in splendour then manifest in the carriage air, a swarm of living nymphalid charms which spurt a stream of shining pearls—

And hold me tight and bear me up on high,
Lend me the whispered majesty of wings,
We'll veil the stars and blaze across the sky,
And shun the wakefulness that morning brings.
When golden boys are aethyr-born, it seems
They rouse the untamed rapture of our dreams.

—the whispered majesty of wings—and more—that dream he had, an impossible host of naked boys in some improbable firmament—and more— they drift with expressions blanked in ecstasy driving their rigid phalluses to issue in the timeless and universal rite which binds them each to the other and all to their forebears—and more—their torrents of falling semen a shower of molten rain—and more—pearlescent downpour he hoped might fall in endless consummation soft and more sweet more and more—soft more limbs down gold hair and more the soft mouth soft sweet flesh and surging spray which spoke to air in a blazing sky—and more—and here—and now—it comes—
—*explosion!*—

Lying entwined in a humid dusk, slicked with cooling sweat, they watched with the others while Trixie Blade performed her bordello party piece.

Pulling down her cotton knickers, she hitched her skirt and lay on a carpet of cushions with her modest penis raised from her shaven crotch. All eyes were fixed on that tremulous hood while it shuddered to the rhythm of her breathing, and the muscles of her legs which flexed themselves until she ejaculated, four long arcs that spattered all over her chest. Luca had been muttering a hex, and he followed the spurts with the pointing bone, quivering the air and arresting one of the ropes of sperm, frozen milk-splash in soft light glittering. He grinned then, pointing still, moved the delicate necklace through the air and held it likea precious fruit above the faces of the entranced company. Each put out their tongues to taste the suspended pearls.

—*susurration in the dark, feline silhouette and rustles of gilded sundering*—'*comes it now then dreams it here and wake to you for you to wake and here it dreams then now it comes*'—

The Paper Lantern

Jon Macy

IT WAS THE MOST DELICIOUS NIGHT, THE NIGHT I FOUND THE CREATURE IN MY GARDEN.

THE AIR SWAM WARM AND BOILED WITH A STRANGE FRAGRANCE.

OR HIS ABILITY TO RETURN TO HIS HOME.

I THOUGHT PERHAPS HE HAD LOST HIS WAY,

IT WASN'T DIFFICULT TO COAX HIM INTO THE HOUSE, BUT HE WAS HUNGRY, AND I HAD NO IDEA WHAT A FAERY WAS WONT TO EAT.

HE WAS FILTHY AS WELL, BUT HE HAD NO ODOR. IN FACT NO MATTER HOW LONG HE WENT WITHOUT A BATH DID HE EVER SMELL AT ALL.

IT WAS LIKE HE DIDN'T EXIST EXCEPT FOR THE LAYER OF EARTH. IT WAS THE ONLY REAL PART OF HIM ONE COULD TOUCH.

THE GRIT ONLY GLISTENED ON HIM AND MADE HIM EVEN MORE BEAUTIFUL. AND HE WAS BEAUTIFUL. A TERRIBLE SWEET BEAUTY THAT COULD BREAK YOUR HEART IN AN INSTANT IF YOU SAW IT UNVEILED. A BRILLIANT SILVER THAT WOULD BLIND YOU IF NOT FOR THE TARNISH.

HE REVELED IN HIS MIRE, GETTING BLACK WITH SOOT, OR DUSTED COMPLETELY WITH GRIME.

THERE WAS NO FOOD OR DRINK THAT HE COULD STOMACH. I EXHAUSTED MY POOR COOK WITH LABORIOUS DISHES AND THE FINEST OF WINES.

HE ONLY WAS FASCINATED BY A CHEAP PAPER LANTERN I HAD BOUGHT ON A WHIM ONE DAY IN CHINA TOWN.

ALTHOUGH HE DID DRINK ALL MY PERFUME.

HOURS WOULD PASS AS IT SPUN SLOWLY, LIGHTING HIS EYES UP LIKE SHARP GOLDEN FLAMES.

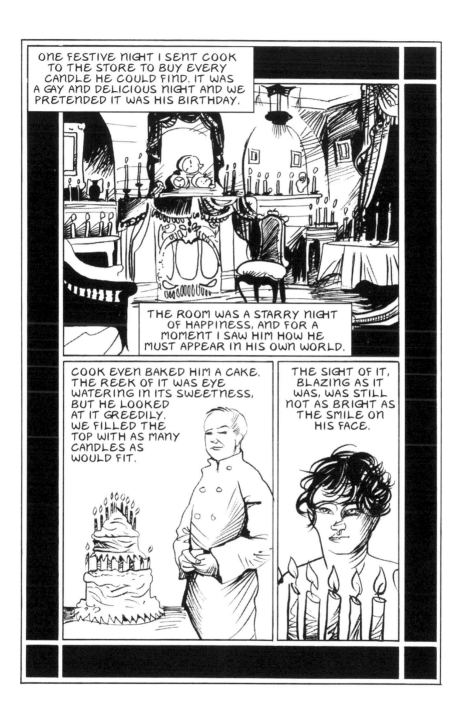

ONE FESTIVE NIGHT I SENT COOK TO THE STORE TO BUY EVERY CANDLE HE COULD FIND. IT WAS A GAY AND DELICIOUS NIGHT AND WE PRETENDED IT WAS HIS BIRTHDAY.

THE ROOM WAS A STARRY NIGHT OF HAPPINESS, AND FOR A MOMENT I SAW HIM HOW HE MUST APPEAR IN HIS OWN WORLD.

COOK EVEN BAKED HIM A CAKE. THE REEK OF IT WAS EYE WATERING IN ITS SWEETNESS, BUT HE LOOKED AT IT GREEDILY. WE FILLED THE TOP WITH AS MANY CANDLES AS WOULD FIT.

THE SIGHT OF IT, BLAZING AS IT WAS, WAS STILL NOT AS BRIGHT AS THE SMILE ON HIS FACE.

85

THEN IT WAS TIME FOR THE WISH, BUT WE COULD NOT CONVEY TO HIM THE NEED TO BLOW OUT THE CANDLES TO RECEIVE THIS SPECIAL GIFT.

HIS GOLDEN EYES STARED LONG AT THE TINY FLAMES UNTIL FINALLY, STICKING OUT HIS POINTED TONGUE, HE ATE EACH ONE IN TURN.

THEY SEEMED TO DISAPPEAR INSIDE HIM CAUSING HIM NO HARM. HE THEN BECAME RAVENOUS AND GORGED HIMSELF ON ALL THE CANDLES IN THE ROOM.

UNTIL AT LAST HE CAME TO THE PAPER LANTERN HE SO LOVED.

THE ROOM WENT DARK. THERE WAS HEARD A MIGHTY CRASH, AND A SCREAM THAT I ASSUMED WAS COOK, AS HE IS QUITE HIGH STRUNG. THEN A GLOW COULD BE SEEN. AND THEN A FLAME.

SOON THE ROOM WAS ABLAZE AND I YELLED "FIRE" AND WE WENT TO GRAB THE WATER BUCKETS, BUT WHEN THE WATER WAS THROWN AND THE FIRE QUENCHED WE SAW NOT A BOY,

BUT A GOLDEN DRAGON.

THE BEAUTY OF IT WAS STARTLING AND I STILL SEE IT MOMENTARILY AGAINST MY EYE LIDS LIKE I HAD STARED TOO LONG AT THE SUN.

IN FACT IT'S THE ONLY THING THAT SOOTHES ME NOW THAT HE'S GONE. I HAVE ALSO TAKEN UP DRINKING PERFUME.

Act II

Modern Monsters

Monster Movie

Rebecca Brown

I LOVED MONSTER movies when I was a kid, and sometimes I still do. The old corny ones more than the new ones: *Frankenstein, Wolfman, Dracula, The Creature From the Black Lagoon.* The little boys I ran around with and I (most girls didn't like monster movies) loved, especially, Lon Chaney and Boris Karloff. We even loved saying their names.

I remember how the Creature from that Black Lagoon had that weird fish mouth, like he was always trying to say something but couldn't or trying to breathe or suck but couldn't either. His eyes were too high on his head and too wide open like he was frightened. Of us? Of himself? Of what he might do with his creepy flesh? Or just surprised like, Why me? Why me? Is this really me?

He looked like any minute he could drown, even if he lived in water. He also couldn't be out of water long. There wasn't any place where he could always be. Something had happened to make him wrong and things weren't right with him. Some of us partly knew some of this, but also there were other things we didn't and didn't want to. He had finny hands and scaly legs and bony, webby feet and a big wide gaping-open toothless wanting mouth. He looked pathetic.

For a while there was a girl in class with skin between her toes. As soon as we heard she did, we made her show us. It looked like webs. When she saw her feet another girl screamed and made a face. The girl wasn't in school very long with us; I think her family moved around a lot.

I also remember Frankenstein, how he lurched around and cried like someone who lived in our neighborhood but who we never saw. I only knew about him because sometimes I heard him crying. It was a sad, wide whine, not crying like tears, but crying more like moaning. Like sounds from someone who couldn't say what it needed to. It sounded like a child except it sounded like a man and then, when I saw the movie, Frankenstein.

Frankenstein lifted his hands toward the light. His sleeves were too short so you could see his skinny, bony wrists. His hands were shaky and pasty white. He looked pathetic too.

In Mary Shelley's *Frankenstein*, I learned when I finally read it in my 20s, the Creature is initially described as, partly, beautiful: "His limbs were in proportion, and I had selected his features as beautiful. Beautiful! - Great God!.... his hair was of lustrous black, and flowing; his teeth of a pearly whiteness..." (Vol 1: chapter IV). The doctor's made him from the best parts of a bunch of different bodies. (What happened to the other parts the doctor didn't choose? What happened to with those bad dismembered bits? What is it to be less than Frankenstein?)

At first the Creature wants to love and be loved by his "father." But when his "father" sees what he's created, he's repulsed. He runs away: "... to avoid the wretch..." Abandoning what he brought forth from pride. Why bring to life a thing you will reject? Why make a thing, belt it, then run out on it? Why make a thing that hates itself? A thing that wishes it were not alive? Who's flawed in this scenario? Whose awful fault is what?

The Wolfman turned to something he couldn't CONTROL. He had to be another thing he was ashamed of. Would he have been alright if he'd been able to live in the woods? I mean without other human beings. I remember him writhing, frothing at the mouth, his legs and stomach clutching and him returning to looking normal as he died.

The Mummy was someone dead who was trying to stay that way, at peace. Sometimes you're gladder there than being alive. But other people wanted to steal his gold and jewels and secret ancient stuff. They were told they shouldn't–there was a curse–but they did it anyway. I remember the creak of the painted sarcophagus opening (I loved it when I learned that word), the giant, shifting shadows on the wall, the weird music. I remember the clutch and the lurch and fall, the body's hurt as it becomes undead. I remember it slowly unwrapping itself, unwinding the limp white cloth that had protected it. It fell away like a tired dress at the end of the day from a girl who doesn't want to do what she's about to do; it falls to the floor.

Mummies were embalmed; they'd had their innards taken out and sometimes they were buried with their cats which, selfish as it was to kill your pet, at least meant you would not be dead alone.

The girls who did like monsters liked Dracula; I didn't as much. Dracula was rich and had everything. He lived in his family's castle and I could tell beneath his soft, calm voice was something that was not. What I did like was that normal people couldn't see him in a mirror; sometimes people can't see people where they look.

There was also the lady with snakes in her hair. I didn't see her in the movies but in my dreams. I dreamt about her all the time for years. I remember half-waking up terrified, trying to get myself fully awake so I could get out of my bed and out of my room and go find my mother to comfort me. At some point she told me that there was a lady in ancient stories named Medusa who had snakes in her hair. Had I heard a story about her somewhere, my mother wanted to know. I must have. Where? Was there something I wanted to tell my mother? She worried. Medusa was, for many years, my in-my-own-head-nightmare-dreaming movie. Was she a monster or something else? Had she been in me forever or just arrived? Was she in me to protect me or to teach me something? Was she warning me? It has been years, now, since I dreamt of her, but I do not forget.

Dr Jekyll and Mr Hyde did not seem monstrous to me. When he changed the way he looked it made it easier because then you would see how he was and try to run away. The bad thing was when you didn't know what to expect and later no one else would believe someone like him had done a thing like that.

I don't remember if I was actually frightened by monster movies or if I just liked that they indicated that someone else knew the world was, in addition to the way it was supposed to be, a weird and creepy place. Sometimes the monsters weren't really monsters but only people something had happened to or who got lost from the far-away place where they were meant to live. A lot of times, if you thought about it, the monsters would have been nice.

One of the things I remember the most from my childhood is an episode of *The Twilight Zone* that was about a sort of monster. I think I even remember the title of it. Which I could look up but I'm not going to because half–maybe more than half–of what's important about what you remember is the way you remember it even if it's not exactly right. The title I remember is "The Eye of the Beholder" and it was about a girl who was really, really ugly, so ugly and deformed–she was repulsive–people couldn't stand to look at her. So these people were going to give her an operation so she could look normal and they wouldn't have to look at her horrible repulsive face any more. The way everyone reacted to her made you think if you looked at her you would throw up but that, because they felt sorry for her, they were nice.

There were a lot of doctors in the episode, and a lot of hushed, earnest talking about the ugly deformed gross hideous girl's repulsiveness. The episode built up to the operation. Then, after the operation, when the result of their attempt to fix the girl is going to be revealed, there was a huge tension as the nice people unwrapped the bandages. This part is shot from the point of view of the girl so you can see the bandages coming off layer by layer. They're gauzy and freeing and loose it was kind of almost beautiful to see.

From the outside, I imagined, the bandages looked like the bandages that came unwrapped in *The Mummy* and *The Curse of the Mummy's Tomb*. In her case, though, you see it from only the inside, from in her, all waiting and hopeful and terrified.

Everything else before this has been shot from behind or above; you've never seen the doctors' or nurses' faces. Then, when at last the mummy bandages are unwrapped, and the doctors and nurses see the girl and–they gasp in horror. She's still completely ugly; she is repulsive. As ugly and gross and hideous and repulsive as she was before. You get nervous they're going to show you her horrible face and you might vomit. But then, when the camera shows her–she's beautiful! Gorgeous! Prettier than any girl in my class and even all of my older sister's pretty, popular friends. She is soooooo pretty! Then the camera moves back and you see, for the first time, the doctors' and nurses' faces and they are ugly. Their lips are fat and twisted and they have huge flaps over their eyes and everything on their faces is bulbous or in a slightly wrong place, deformed, and they look gross.

You cover your eyes. How did you not notice, while it was happening, the camera never showed you how the normal people looked?

You cover your eyes.

Girls around are squealing and laughing. You feel hot and stupid and something else and you run from the room.

That night, my older sister–she was high school–was having a slumber party. A lot of her popular, pretty friends were over and they were watching TV and rolling their hair and practicing cheers and talking about boys. Because they thought I was funny and sweet, and because I was young enough they could act like grown ups with me (which I kind of thought they were), they let me hang around with them.

I ran from the room where the TV was and into the bedroom my sister and I shared. But one of my sister's friends was in there changing into her pajamas and didn't have any clothes on which when I saw I stopped and gawped at then turned around and ran away again but there was nowhere else to go. Where could I hide?

I was too young to talk about boys but I wouldn't have anyway.

I didn't know that then; did they? Would they have known the thing I was if they had seen me?

American Dreams

Ocean Vuong

Baby, we made it. We're riding in the back
of the black limousine.
The crowd along the road shouting
our names. Cameras, lights,
cyanide. The crowd surrounded
by so much freedom and
ambulances. They have faith
in your golden hair and crisp blue suit.
They have a good citizen
in me. I love my country. I pretend
nothing is wrong. I pretend
not to see the man and his daughter
ducking for cover, that you're not saying
my name and it's not coming out
like a slaughterhouse. I'm not really
Jackie-O and you're not JFK
and there isn't a hole in your head,
a brief rainbow through a mist
of red. But who am I kidding?
I'm holding your brains in, darling,
my sweet, sweet Jack. I'm reaching
across the trunk for a shard
of your memory, the one
where we kiss and the room
goes dark. Your slumped back.
Your hand letting go. You're all over
the car now, deepening
my fuchsia dress. I'm a good
citizen, surrounded by God
and ambulances. *I love
my country*, I keep saying. *I love
my country*. The twisted faces. *I love
my country*. The blue sky. Black
limousine. My one white glove
glistening pink—with all
your American dreams.

B.E.M.s

Gregory L. Norris

A VERY WISE man once said—and I paraphrase—that if you live by the sword, there's a good chance you'll die by it. I wonder if the same holds true for the stake. Or the cock. Because sooner or later, my dick's gonna do me in.

My name is August Rensallier, and like a lot of hopeful actors, I came to Tinsel Town to be discovered. Two seasons ago, I snagged the lead in a gothic Science Fiction series broadcast on the Alphabet Network. *The Night Staker* is cheeseball at its lowest moments, genius in its best. It survived the ax at the end of its first year on the air. Halfway through the second, while smoking a coffin nail in the back alley behind Studio 17 where *Staker* is filmed, I got discovered again, by a whole different kind of audience. The B.E.M.s.

His name was Ethan Maynard Tenderly. Kid had acted in bit guest parts on *His Father, the Bicycle* and one memorable episode of *The Few Likes of Toby Willis*, as Willis's new best buddy from college, who tended to mince about a lot theatrically. He stood close to the six-foot mark, his body that of a swimmer's, his hands and feet just slightly too long for the rest of his build, but you got the sense his body would even out in a few years, maybe five, after life and this town toughened him.

Only Ethan Tenderly didn't have five years. Probably didn't have five minutes, given the smell of B.E.M.s in the air on that fourth day of filming Episode 3:23, "The Decay of Light and Substance."

Our first scenes that morning, filmed in the office of Jeremy Saturn, the Night Staker, were difficult enough without the cloying orchid scent that starts off sweet and hypnotic, dazes your brain so you let down your guard. There had to be three, maybe four of them close by. Close enough to smell. Since I started staking B.E.M.s, I choke on the pheromones they exude. A small pack, hungry to feed. Fuck a duck.

Tenderly was pretty; B.E.M.s love their meals handsome and innocent. I struggled to deliver my lines.

"They're close," I/Saturn said.

Tenderly, in the role of Troy Tanner, Young Man with a Terrible Secret, asked, "Who's close, Mister Saturn?"

"The fucking bug-eyed monsters, that's who."

Silence, then Bernie Coltrane, the episode's director, yelled, "*Cut.*"

"Bug-eyed monsters?" chuckled Tenderly. "You mean 'the Psycho-vamps'?"

Saturn's sworn enemies, devourers of bodies and souls in the make-believe world of *The Night Staker*. "Sure, yeah, them," I lied.

A minute later, we were back in form. The olfactory ooze of the real enemy had thickened. So had the bone in my pants.

"Mister Saturn, you're my only hope," Tenderly/Tanner pleaded.

I gazed into the handsome young man's pale eyes, blue leaning toward gray, and recorded the quiver of his lower lip for future jerk-off fantasies.

It struck me that I, not Saturn, was his only hope. I gripped the Holy Prop, Necravarian, and nodded. "Meet me in my trailer. Bernie, we're taking ten."

"What? *Now?* You nailed that scene, you and the kid. For Chrissake, Ren—!"

"Ren?" Tenderly said.

"Only the crew call me 'Ren'—guest stars call me *August.*"

Tenderly shook free of my grip. "Okay, August."

I popped a smoke into my mouth and studied him through narrowed eyes and the first smoky exhale. "I think I prefer 'Mister Rensallier' from you."

Tenderly folded his arms and assumed a cocky stance, his body language impossible to misread. Part of me wanted to smack the pout off his face. The rest considered crushing my mouth over it. That whole dick-trouble thing again—and mine was up at the notion of such a kiss.

"Do you smell that?" I asked.

Tenderly shrugged. "You mean that noxious cigarette clamped between your lips?"

I stabbed the smoke out and waved the air. "The orchids."

"That old lady perfume? I thought—"

"Listen carefully to me. You're a smart young man, so be sure you use your thinking cap. Somewhere not far from where you and I are standing, here and now, are evil beings from another dimension intent on killing you. Devouring you alive, in fact. Sucking your marrow out of your bones and picking their teeth with your toenails."

Tenderly made a face. "The Psycho-vamps?"

"No, but they're a lot like them. I think that's why they started showing up on the studio lot, though. This goddamn TV show—maybe they think it's real, and that Jeremy Saturn's out to get them, their mortal enemy. The prop—"

I picked up Necravarian, Saturn's holiest-of-holies, the relic from Transylvania he used to stake and slay the Psycho-vamps on the small screen. One jab, and the evil creatures caught fire and evaporated, courtesy of the special effects department in post-production. The same stake's delivery was considerably messier in the real world.

"Touch it," I ordered.

"I beg your pardon?" Tenderly said. Then he understood the thing I intended for him to grope was Necravarian. "Oh, the Night Staker's stake."

"What did you think I meant?"

"That suspicious-looking bulge in your pocket," he fired back.

I drew my jacket aside enough to show him that the bulge was a snub-nosed revolver. Tenderly gasped again.

".38 Special, with silver bullets—they work wonders against those bug-eyed sonsabitches, too."

The young actor smiled, and part of me surrendered to territory I wasn't ready to relinquish. "Is this some kind of joke? You know, like a fraternity initiation on set? Me being the new guy and all."

"No, because if you don't listen to me, you're going to be the *dead* guy on set. They love your type."

Defenses again sprang up. "My type?"

"Yeah, kid."

"You don't mean—?"

"Young, full of dreams, still innocent. They like their victims pretty, which is why they're here in Tinsel Town sucking down souls and dreams. As for the queer part, I don't think they really care. I'll give them credit for that, the boogly-eyed bastards."

"Look," Tenderly barked.

"No, you look."

I seized his hand, forced Necravarian into his grip, and waited. Breaths labored and grew louder on both sides. Our fingers met on the shaft of the holy weapon—in the canon of *The Night Staker*, Necravarian was hewn from the crossbar of the Crucified Christ. Part of me wondered if that part, too, might be real, given the way it made B.E.M.s blow apart like frogs full of lit firecracker.

Electricity crackled at contact, invisible yet there, recorded via emotion. Our eyes again met. In that bottled gaze, I couldn't be sure if our conversation passed through words or telepathy.

"There are sinister forces at work out there. Hungry beings. *Deadly.* If you trust me, you might just survive for a return appearance. Now tell me, do you feel anything?"

"No," he rasped, his voice husky, dry. I knew it was a lie. "Only disappointment."

He released Necravarian, about-faced, and marched out of my trailer.

And into mortal danger.

Live by the dick, die by it, truly. Mine stuck out like a divining rod, pointing not toward water but Ethan Tenderly—and the pack of bug-eyed devils readying to devour him somewhere close by in the studio back lot.

I've learned a lot of lessons playing Jeremy Saturn. Up is sometimes down. A stage prop can wield more energy than an A-bomb. Some guest stars are worth risking your life over. And that it's never smart to get cocky, because the B.E.M.s, whoever or whatever they are, are monsters regardless of where they originate.

Three figures approached Tenderly.

"Hello," he said, oblivious to the drooling, clacking jaws spilling saliva over him, or the gelatinous foreheads full of rheumy, unblinking eyes.

I hoped contact with Necravarian would illuminate Tenderly, as it had me. I gripped the holy weapon and hurried to catch up.

"*Saturn*," the B.E.M. closest to Tenderly bellowed in a voice spoken through a clotted filter of phlegm.

"Saturn? It's Rensallier, you idiot," I said and, seeing they had Tenderly under their spell, doing that trick with the eyes, I marched right up and drove the tip of Necravarian between the fucker's multitude of peepers.

The salivating punk instantly melted into reds and greens and your less-tasty shades of vomit. Some of it, regrettably, splashed poor Tenderly, right in his pretty mug. He came out of the trance and screamed. I slashed at the next B.E.M. with a lower cut, then threw an upper at the third, nailing it where humans have hearts. B.E.M. Three followed B.E.M. One onto the asphalt, reduced to a puddle of puke. My slash across B.E.M. Two's midriff had liquefied its lower half. The upper hissed and scrambled toward the young actor, eyeballs now standing out on stalks and the reason behind Tenderly's shrieks.

"Jeepers fucking creepers. Oh, for the love of Lassie," I spat, and finished the top half off with a hard stab through the forehead.

The smell of orchids and old ladies grew suffocating. Puddles of vanquished monsters steamed in the noonday sun. By the end of lunch break, those remains would evaporate fully, gone into the ether.

I shook off Necravarian, tried to not think of the image that activity always conjured in my dirty mind—that of standing at a urinal, post drain.

"What-?" Tenderly asked in a voice barely above a whisper, having screamed himself hoarse. "What the fuck where those things?"

"I told you."

"B.E.M.s?" he asked.

"My little pet nickname. They could be space men or interstellar space trash, vampires, shape shifters, creatures from the La Brea tar pits. Hell, maybe they're Hollywood agents—they certainly love to feast upon the innocent and talented with gusto. I don't know for sure. They never stick around long enough for chit chat."

"Bug-eyed monsters," Tenderly said.

And then he fainted into my arms.

I dabbed at his forehead with a handkerchief run under the icy water from the cooler in my trailer. Up close, Tenderly's angelic beauty struck me with the force of a punch to the guts. I could see why the B.E.M.s salivated over him. I wanted to devour Ethan Tenderly, too.

He stirred, mewled. My hunger worsened at this image of his eyes fretting behind lids and the way his mouth twisted in a frown. Not yet conscious, he leaned into my touch. I stroked his hair. Tenderly drifted out of the fugue.

"Mister Rensallier?"

An unfamiliar gesture tugged at the corners of my mouth, too—the first genuine smile I could remember since the first night I crossed paths with the B.E.M.s, what now felt a thousand light years in my past.

"Shhh," I soothed, another rarity. I'm not the nurturing sort. Only with Tenderly, I wanted to be.

He woke fully against my palm. Our eyes connected, and whatever specters chased him in his sleep were slain. Then he jolted up.

"Those things—!"

"Dead. Staked. But you can bet your bottom dollar there are more of them out there—and that they'll be back, looking for you."

He considered my words, choked down a swallow. I walked over to the water cooler and filled a paper cone. Tenderly drank. My imagination wandered back into sweaty territory.

"So what are we to do?"

"*We?*" I parroted.

"Yes, you and I."

He placed his hand over mine. The rush of bullish emotion, brief but red-hot, shorted out, driven apart by a brisk shiver. The chill tumbled down my spine. The room phased out of focus. And like a dream sequence flashback from *The Night Staker*, there I was again, screaming and bleeding, being savaged by horrors from another dimension.

"*There is something wrong with your television set,*" the mellifluous voice reported. "*Try and adjust the horizontal, the vertical. You are no longer in control. Don't sit there—run…run! And pray you see him before they find you. This is the Night Staker…*"

I'd gone out there, angry and exhausted, still had the stupid prop in my hands. Episode Seven, Season One—"*The Architects of Madness.*" I despise that fucking episode. Hated it even before that cigarette break found me in the back alley, outside my trailer. Live by the coffin nail, die by it, only I didn't. Came close, though.

I lit the smoke, dragged a hit, exhaled it out of my nostrils. Through the curlicues of smoke and the question marks they formed in the darkness,

I remembered Bernie's words before the break, after which it was hoped I'd get my shit together. "Put your soul into it. Act like you're scared—really goddamn piss-your-pants terrified, Ren!"

I gripped Necravarian, Jeremy Saturn's trusted weapon against the evil Psycho-vamps. Stupid episode. Stupid TV show. The hour grew later, and I still had yet to nail the scene. My heart wasn't in it, let alone my soul. After Korea, staking rubber-suit monsters with plastic fangs and bugged-out eyes barely quickened my pulse.

Another deep drag. Among the smoke, I detected a cloying sweetness in the air, a smell of flowers, growing stronger with each breath. *Orchids?* Though comforting at first, even challenging my frustration, the perfume fouled on the next sip of air, worsening my mood. The odor painted my taste buds with an oily residue of funerals, dark rooms, and killing frosts. I thought about giving up the cigarettes. Then Necravarian, the holy relic, grew hot in my hand, so much so that my instinct was to pitch the damn thing, like a baseball.

I took aim, but saw two men standing in the shadows cast over the alley by the brick wall. Their eyes crawled over my flesh. I figured them for stagehands or fans who'd hopped the fence.

"Take a picture—it'll last longer," I said.

Two men, with unblinking gazes. Only as they marched forward, I saw they weren't men.

"Is this some kind of fucking joke?" I demanded. I wasn't in the mood, but had to admit the makeup department had done a hell of a job. "Tell Bernie I don't need any help getting into character."

"Fuck Bernie, Saturn," one of the two bug-eyed freaks burbled and smacked his chops. "You make my mouth water."

"Go suck Senator McCarthy's dead dick," I spat.

It was years after Low-Blow Joe's Hollywood witch hunt, but even in 1962 you couldn't be too safe, especially when strange feelings crossed paths with the easy smorgasbord of flesh that is Tinsel Town.

"You're more our type," the second monster snorted. "We can't leave you running around, staking our kind through the heart. You're going to taste so yummy in my tummy, Saturn!"

"My name's not really—" I started, but got no further, because at that moment they jumped me.

Filthy teeth tore into my shoulder, bit through my jacket, my shirt, my skin. Pain flared, exquisite in its intensity. I took a bullet's graze in Korea. That was nothing like being snacked on by B.E.M.s, the—

"—dirty punks." I sighed smoke through my nostrils and showed Tenderly the scar.

His eyes widened. My shirt hung open, one side shrugged off my shoulder. It wasn't often that I was able to force myself to face the scar directly, whether in the mirror when I shaved or on those few occasions when I fucked, so I understood the kid's reaction. He reached tentatively toward it, his long, lean fingers quivering. I tried to not think about how magical his touch would feel on other parts of a man's anatomy.

"Does it hurt?"

I shook my head. "Not anymore. Go ahead."

His fingertips settled on the chewed topography of my shoulder and wandered over scar tissue.

"What did you do?"

Snorting a laugh, I said, "I staked the fuckers, that's what."

His focus wandered to Necravarian, the holy TV show prop, then back up to my eyes, taking a detour along my chest, freshly-shaved courtesy of the hair and makeup department for the looming beefcake calendar scene in tomorrow's section of the shooting script.

"The thing's real, either that or they believe it is. I asked our prop guy. Said he found it in a junk shop near Toluca Lake. Thing is, I think there's something bigger at work here."

"Bigger?"

I fell deeper into Tenderly's eyes and, for the first time, it was easier to speak that particular sobriquet. "Yeah. *Destiny.*"

A knock sounded on the door. "Ren? Ren? You in there?" called Bernie Coltrane.

I pulled my shirt on as much as possible on the march to the trailer's door. Nothing would make it look like I hadn't been tumbling around back there with some choice piece of tail, so I didn't bother tucking in tails.

"Yeah, Bernie?"

Through the door, he answered, "Any chance you might grace us with your presence during President Kennedy's term in office?"

I cracked the door. A noxious puff of gray smoke off Bernie's stogie drifted through the gap. I fanned my face.

"I mean, not to be too much of a tyrant and all, but I'd appreciate getting at least one frame of useable film in today. Or, should we get so lucky, a whole scene in the can, if you wouldn't mind getting a move on it."

"Okay, Bernie. Christ."

He tipped his eyes in the direction of the water cooler and sofa, the latter presently occupied by my new friend. "Seen anything of our young guest star?"

"Maybe."

Bernie sucked on the cigar, nodded, exhaled. "We'd appreciate seeing him on stage, too, if you'd be so kind as to pass the message along."

"Give me a minute."

"As Brubek said in '59, take five." Bernie turned back toward the entrance to Studio 17, completely oblivious to the recent turf war that had taken place on the sun-blanched asphalt beneath his loafers.

Soft footsteps scuffled behind me. I spun around. Tenderly looked pale and unsteady on his legs.

"What do I do?" he asked.

"What you have to. Channel the terror into your performance. Go out there and wow them with your acting. And for the love of all that's holy, you smell orchids, run as fast as you can!"

He took to the stage. Blood around the set ran cold.

"I saw them, too, Saturn," Troy/Tenderly said, eyes wide, sweat glistening on his brow and dripping from the tips of his blond cowlicks. And then his voice rose to a shriek. "Those bloodsucking devils, they're real! They're out there! They're—"

Tenderly screamed.

Fade out.

"You nailed it," I said.

Tenderly had turned the day around following his nightmarish encounter on the back lot, but the praise from cast and crew did little to alleviate the new worry lines around his eyes, likely permanent now that he'd taken a good long look into the bad truth.

"It nailed me," he said, loosening his thin black tie. Nimble fingers worked open the top button of his white shirt. Perspiration dampened a ring around the collar, I saw.

I wanted to hug him, tell him that everything would be all right, only it would be a lie. A sweet nothing meant to satisfy my carnal needs.

His eyes dropped to my waist. "Any chance you'll loan me that suspicious-looking bulge for the long walk home?"

"Huh?" I asked.

"Your snub-nosed revolver. Your gun."

I shifted from one foot to the other. "Oh, that? That bulge isn't my gun," I said, and offered to see him safely home.

Like I said, this dick of mine's gonna get me killed.

Tenderly lived in a rented room on Sepulveda. The only artwork on the wall was your typical paint-by-number landscape. The sheets smelled of bleach. What little belonged to him was neatly arranged in two suitcases, one of which sat open on a luggage rack. A trench coat hung from a wooden coat tree, beneath a man's hat that would have looked great on any hardboiled TV detective's head. Probably better on Ethan Tenderly's, I imagined.

"Nice place," I said.

"Thanks, but you don't have to lie."

I glanced into his open suitcase at the neat rows of boxers and balls of socks. "I wasn't."

"Until I land something regular, it's the best I can afford."

"We all make due and suffer for our art."

Tenderly closed the door beneath an open transom and waved me toward the only other furniture upon which to sit apart from the bed, a chair near the desk that also served as dining room table. I took the chair backwards in that classic stance of cowboys and tough guys. It creaked and complained beneath the muscles of my ass.

"I guess we've both suffered on that count," he said, and sat on the edge of the bed.

I didn't respond. An answer wasn't necessary. Our eyes met. Whole conversations passed unspoken in that bottled gaze.

"So…is there someone special?" he eventually asked.

"Yes," I said, forcing a wounded puppy dog look upon his gaze. "Necravarian."

A measure of joy surged back. "*You*," he laughed, all nerves. "I meant—"

"No."

"A pity."

"Why's that?"

"Because…"

He never finished the thought, and instead slid off the corner of the mattress, his movements liquid, elegant, impossible to resist. On his knees, he glanced up, cupped my cheeks with both hands, those long, incredible hands, and, saying nothing more, crushed his lips against mine.

Live by the dick, die by the dick.

I kissed back hard, gripped his neck, dropped my guard, let down the invisible walls constructed since Jeremy Saturn became the man, August Rensallier the actor. For a long while, I hadn't allowed myself the possibility of love; didn't buy it even at that moment while forcing my tongue between his lips, demanding he surrender more territory to my lust. But I considered it.

I rose from the chair, pulling Tenderly up with me. I tossed him onto the bed, undressed him first with eyes, fingers next. Naked and erect before me, all mine, I also considered the possibility of the Divine in my vulnerable new state. As I learned a decade earlier when I was eighteen in Korea, '53, there are no atheists in the battle trenches. Or at twenty-eight in rented bedrooms where the finest of the fine hang their trench coats and hats.

"Magnificent," I growled.

Tenderly sat up and reached for my belt. "I was thinking the same thing."

What followed was both less and more than I expected. Less in that halfway into corkscrewing his ass, I realized this was it: I was ruined for life, and no other pretty Hollywood face would ever measure up to Ethan Tenderly. More, because I understood that my butt wasn't the only one in need of protection. From this night forward, I had to defend Ethan Maynard Tenderly from becoming tartare to those bug-eyed fucks.

A corn-fed Midwestern boy, I learned. Youngest of five sons, his family Oklahoma farmers. While the rest of his siblings batted around baseballs, Ethan read books, watched the television, and dreamed of a bigger world. Just how big, he hadn't guessed until his encounter in the back alley.

"And you?"

I kissed the top of his head, tasted the cooling post-coitus sweat conjured from our second tumble. "California, born and bred."

I told him about the war, the bullet, and how, upon my return to the States via Japan, a military photographer's snapshot led to my first gig as a walk-on on the live TV show, *Mystery Cavalcade Theatre*. A bit part on a serial that jumped from radio to the tube followed. Roles on episodes of *The Twilight Gallery* and *The Outer Orbit*, and then one afternoon the telephone rang.

"And behold—*The Night Staker*."

I twirled one of Tenderly's cowlicks. Fuck, I could get used to this. But then he had to ruin it.

"What about the B.E.M.s?"

"What about them?"

He fixed me with an accusing look. "Those things are out there, eating people alive. Don't you think it's time we found out what they really are, what they want?"

"I know what they are, what they want. Sick, slimy sonsabitches, hungry to suck face and choke down intestines."

"No, I mean the bigger plan."

I'd asked myself similar questions, once upon a time. Clearly, happiness—like any level of success in Tinsel Town—always comes with a price.

"Can we shelve the bigger plans for the night? Morning comes early at Studio 17."

He grunted something beneath his breath and broke focus. "Goodnight."

"Night."

He rolled over. I grabbed a handful of his bare ass. Tenderly chuckled. It felt like ownership. It felt fairly fucking great. I wasn't used to the emotion, but exhaustion soon claimed me in a strange bed, beside a stranger I wanted to know better.

I rolled over in the darkness, convinced I was back in Korea, bleeding from the gunshot graze, only a B.E.M. had pulled the trigger. My heart attempted to throw itself into my throat. Mercifully, it clogged up the works, and the scream building in my chest log-jammed behind the lump, silenced as I struggled for breath. The bald light filtering down through the transom above the door reestablished the boundaries of Tenderly's rented room.

I swung my legs out from under the covers, saw stars as my erection took an awkward roll across the top sheet, smelled the stale remains of passionate sex between two men.

"Ethan," I called.

The bunched bedclothes on the other side of the mattress didn't answer. I slipped out of bed and found the light switch.

Ethan Tenderly was gone. So was his trench coat and Joe-cool detective's hat.

Most telling, so was Necravarian.

I stuffed my dick into my pants and zipped up.

"You crazy fucking do-gooder," I huffed.

I pulled on the rest of my duds and exited the rented room, not knowing which way to turn, where to find him. Grunting a blue-streak beneath my breath, I hot-footed it onto Sepulveda and walked.

My soles had covered a lot of ground in Tinsel Town, but never so much as on that night. From Sepulveda to Hollywood Boulevard, from Hollywood to a seedy little back road called North Whitley. Rancid citrus smells from lemons and oranges left to rot on the ground mixed with fouler orchids. I was on the right track.

I checked the snub-nosed, grabbed my dick by mistake, found it just as steely. My breaths burned in my throat. My sweat exuded the sourness of raw nerves and dirty ashtrays. They were nearby, somewhere in the tangle of concrete rat trap apartments and bungalows. North Whitley. I started up the sidewalk, aware of two important observations: one, the silence; two, the darkness, the total absence of all light save for the pale fluorescent glow emanating from a front window in one of those apartment houses, a television running on snow.

This was a B.E.M. stronghold, for sure. Why would those boogly-eyed punks worry about harvesting lemons before they rotted on the branch or ground? They didn't eat citrus. They only snacked on fruit of the human variety.

My anger matched my terror in equal volume—they'd taken my Ethan into that dank place.

My Ethan?

I dug in my heels, reached for a smoke. Lighting the coffin nail added the only other spark of light to the forsaken neighborhood. For the first time, the cigarette tasted noxious, like a dead skunk had crawled onto my tongue. I spit it out and stamped it flat under my shoe. Maybe it was the putrid mix of citrus and B.E.M.s, or that I'd tasted a different new level of fear, one born not from my own terror over death but the death of a life more precious.

Cigarettes, I guessed, would always taste like this from here on forward. If so, I'd do without them. I'd find enjoyment in other pleasures, like Ethan Tenderly. First, I had to rescue him.

I reached down, grabbed the proper bulge—the snub-nosed—for reassurance. Then I honked the other, just because. Time to channel Jeremy Saturn.

"I'm coming, babe," I growled, drew my piece, and entered the stronghold of the enemy.

The joint reeked of stale sweat, rot, and orchids, the mix so thick it could choke an army of dicks. The dreamy, strobing light from the television set drew me into a front parlor. The set was big and boxy, an ugly thing on wooden legs with rabbit ears, running snow after the station played the National Anthem and signed off for the night.

The room stunk, too. Only after seeing the static on the tube did the sensation slithering over my flesh register. This should have been a very normal vignette—TV on braided rug, with checked curtains drawn across window against the night. A classic American slice of life. The American dream. Well, apart from the ratty old davenport soaked in glistening gore, and the picked-clean skeleton propped on the cushions, its vacant sockets aimed at the snowy screen.

"*Ethan,*" I gasped.

The TV screen crackled. Moody Theremin music drifted out of the speakers, similar to the *Night Staker*'s opening theme.

"Mister Saturn," said an ominous voice neither fully male nor female but in a register that suggested both.

I faced the TV. An image formed in the static, that of the ugliest bug-eyed fuck I'd encountered since Necravarian stole the scales from my eyes. Saliva dripped from its clacking jaws. Its multitude of eyes glistened in crystal-clear black and white definition.

"I'm not Sa—" I started, but bit down on the sentence before it could be finished.

Because I *was* that guy.

I truly was the Night Staker.

"You know me," I said. "So you know I'm gonna pound your hide into ketchup for what you did to my friend."

I tipped my chin at the sofa, shocked by the sudden absence of rage or all-consuming hurt. Ice had smothered my emotions.

"That? Oh, that wasn't sweet, tender Ethan Tenderly, Saturn," the sneering, salivating face said, adding a villainous cackle. "Just some tasty morsel we snacked on in anticipation of your arrival. It's so rude to dine in front of company."

A blast of heat shot up from my dick and thawed my frozen insides. "He's alive?"

The image altered in a ripple of vertical zigzags. The bars faded. In their place was Ethan, stripped to the waist, manacled to a filthy cement wall.

"B.E.M.s," he called out. And then his voice rose to a shriek. "*B.E.M.s!*"

His eyes bugged out, though not nearly as widely as those of the two ugly fucks cackling and flapping their filthy forked tongues at his perspiring flesh.

"Leave him alone!" I bellowed.

The angle on the broadcast image canted, zoomed close up, right to Ethan's eyes. More screams filtered out of the idiot tube.

"I'll do anything you want," I said and meant it. "*Anything!*"

The picture zoomed out. The Ugliest of Uglies replaced Ethan on the screen. My Ethan.

"There's a room at the back of the hallway," it said. "Go there and surrender your weapon."

I walked out of the room, followed the hallway into darkness, through a set of disgusting plastic flaps, the kind that hang on the doors of meat lockers. The smell of despair and death burned in my lungs.

"Drop it, Saturn!" one of the two B.E.M.s inside barked.

I dangled my .38 Special from my thumb and faced the freakish sort of set design that put the craziest of *The Night Staker* episodes to shame: a handsome young star manacled to grimy, soundproof walls; two bug-eyed horrors, salivating around jagged smiles, one holding Necravarian in hands covered by fluffy oven gloves; the biggest fucking camera on rusted, rolling casters I'd ever seen, complete with matching teleprompter.

"Welcome to our studio, Saturn," the control voice from the TV taunted from inside the camera. The teleprompter cast the words on a section of wall. "The gun—"

I dropped it.

"Now kick it over," the B.E.M. not holding Necravarian ordered.

I launched it with the toe of my shoe, right at my beautiful Ethan's feet. Our eyes met, and more of that strange telepathy passed between us.

The B.E.M. reached down to retrieve my revolver. As it did, Ethan stomped on its head, reminding me how limber he was in his bed at the rented room on Sepulveda. A sickening crunch bounced off the soundproofing. The B.E.M. burbled an expletive. Ethan toed the gun back in my direction. I ran forward, scooped up my snub-nosed, and fired. Oven Gloves came apart in a gooey cascade of condiment colors, leaving soiled mitts and the holy relic lolling atop a pile of steaming offal.

The other B.E.M. recovered from Ethan's punt and lunged, knocking the gun out of my grasp.

"August!" called Ethan.

The world erupted in a supernova of Technicolor as the impact shoved my spine into the camera's cold metal hide.

"Destroy him!" the control voice screamed. "Destroy Jeremy Saturn!"

The B.E.M. opened its filthy mouth. What I smelled confirmed what I'd come to believe about the bug-eyed cannibals since setting foot on North Whitley, a moment of clarity right before the perceived moment of my death.

Death. Despair. The heart-killing slaughter of dreams mixed with a dose of bloodthirsty desperation for success. The B.E.M.s weren't extraterrestrial in origin—they were Tinsel Town born and bred, a manifestation of the residue of all who'd come here with stars in their eyes but who'd died in the black hole vortex of shattered hope. Jealous horrors hungry for the flesh of pretty up-and-coming talent.

"Yum," the B.E.M. hissed, and readied to bite.

Its flesh ripped apart, and the B.E.M. dissolved in a fountain of foul juices that splashed over my face. I gagged, spit, and wiped the gore from my eyes. A figure formed on the other side of the putrid veil.

"August?" asked Ethan, freed of his manacles.

He held Necravarian, the holy relic, in both hands.

I rose to my feet, took a shaky step forward. "Kid, how-?"

Ethan shrugged. "The cuffs loosened after I launched that kick. My hands are so freakishly long, they just slipped free."

"Maybe. And maybe it was something more."

We both zeroed in on Necravarian, which glowed in the light cast by the sinister camera and teleprompter. Perhaps there was something to that whole 'Destiny' thing after all. Then we embraced.

"Don't you ever put me through that kind of Hell again," I growled into his ear.

"Don't you ever make me," Ethan said in a tone that indicated he'd dug in his heels. "These hideous monsters have to be stopped."

"These monsters are us," I said.

Ethan pulled back, his eyes filled with questions. Before I could answer a single one, the control voice drove us apart with an alien snicker.

"Very clever, Saturn. You understand the situation."

I faced the camera. "You mean about your origins? Finally, yes, I know what you are. *Why* you are."

"Then you know we'll always be out there chewing up the scenery, you could say. Taking our revenge on the industry and its players."

I fixed the lens with a look. "And you know that Jeremy Saturn, the Night Staker will be out there as well, stopping your evil plans at every turn. Remember that!"

I guided Ethan behind the safety of my back, aimed the snub-nosed filled with silver, and fired. The monstrous camera and teleprompter came apart in a shower of sparks and TV snow, that particular broadcast cancelled.

I shut off the water cooler's spout and raised the paper cone to my lips. "What's the good news, Bernie."

"The news is great, in fact. Ratings on last week's episode went through the roof. The network is very, very happy. They're talking about bringing in a love interest for Jeremy Saturn—seems there's romance in the Night Staker's future. The producers want your input. You can have any starlet you want."

I drained the cone, crushed it into a paper baseball, and pitched it at the pail. "Love interest, huh? Anyone I want? I have a better idea. Let's give Saturn a sidekick. How about that Ethan Tenderly guy?"

Live by the dick?

Life sure was looking sunnier, B.E.M.s and all.

The Mighty Mermen

Levi Hastings

Thangs

Imani Sims

I TOLD MY mama an'nem that he wasn't gon' make it. He may be a vampire but his thinking he could hop cross buildings and not mis-step is his own damn fault. Hmph. I tell you them damn immortals, so cocky. Just cuz he gots supernatural thangs doesn't mean he IS supernatural. Thangs is different from being. We all gots thangs.

"Silly man," Patrice said as she rolled her eyes and recounted the story to the shocked crowd. "He came flying through the door of the Tavern talking about we should pay him a nickel to come see him cheat death." Sirens fade in slowly from a distance. Patrice continues, "You know the Carson brothers just laughed and laughed, them big bellies jiggling right over top they jeans. Beer foam caught in they 'staches." Patrice looks briefly back towards the body impaled on the tree just outside the window. The police had begun to assess the scene. The crowd inside the Tavern waited for her to continue.

"They were the first to put money on the table. 'You down right crazy,' they say, 'we'll give you a whole dollar if you can prove you cheat death.' 'Alright,' Mr. Bill say, his cold dead hands gripping the money, 'I'm going to land in air. That's right, in a pocket I build with my own arms and the trees are going to catch me.' The bar erupted with laughter at his cockiness. I just stared at him, deciding whether or not to take part 'n this r'diculous stunt." Patrice continued, "by this time, mutters began to fill the cheeks of women in last night's dresses and rolled over top lips of the quiet man that sits in the corner ever Wends'day. Me, I just looked. Calmly walked up to Mr. Bill and said, here's my nickel, I wanna see you do it."

Muttering slightly under her breath, "funny how one dollar and five cents proved his thangs ain't no better than ours."

The Door

Jeremy Halinen

Opportunity is darting away like a mosquito that has just sucked blood from your best friend and has no immediate need for you. Engorged, off she buzzes with her proboscis and tiny, veined wings. Opportunity is ambling away like a vampire who has just quenched his thirst with your best friend's blood and couldn't care less about your arterial motifs. Off into the night he ventures, fangs drenched, heart warmed. Opportunity is stomping away like your best friend's wife, who has just stabbed him in the back for sleeping with you, leaving him for dead inside you. Off she storms with her knife dripping, and you know she'll never be back. But look: already starting to dry on the door, isn't that the familiar red of your best friend?—testament, perhaps, to a reverse Passover, sign of a new covenant deflowered by a used god who wants nothing to do with you.

Alexander's Wrath

JL Smither

SYDNEY JUMPED WHEN the door to the British Museum Library and Reading Room slammed open and a man strode in with thunderclouds across his brow. The greener soldiers sat up in their cots to stare at him, looming and terrifying in his lupanoid cloak. He passed swiftly among their beds, making eye contact with no one, focusing on the far wall of the circular room. The cloak covered his head with the wolf-like top jaw and face of a lupanoid with sewed-shut eyes, and the beast's thick brown fur draped over his shoulders and back. Its lifeless tail, dark with a white tuft on the end, swayed between his calves. He held this hooded cape together at his breast bone with a man's belt buckle, simple and inexpensive, in sharp contrast to the elaborate skin.

The more seasoned soldiers, those who had been around since the lupanoid crisis started not long after the Blitz just 6 years ago, looked away and nudged the newer recruits to focus back on their card games, books, and letters. Not all of them could.

As Sydney stared at the man who walked toward two empty cots at the back of the room, Lieutenant Thomas Wyndham stepped directly in front of him and blocked his view. Sydney looked up into the face of his commanding officer, who shook his head in warning before turning back toward his own cot.

Sydney lowered his eyes and tried to pick up his interrupted train of thought. He had been writing a letter to his childhood best friend, his sometimes more than friend, who had emigrated after being denied service in the Confrontation. Sydney hadn't even found out until he received a letter postmarked Suez during his first deployment on Hampstead Heath. *A wife*, he had said, *and children. Necessary. A normal life. Away from…* Sydney had shed hot tears.

The hum of conversation gradually began again in the Reading Room, bouncing softly off the blue-and-gold domed ceiling, which gave an outrageous elegance to their sleeping cots, Confrontation-issue blankets, black uniforms, and tranquilizer guns. Their leaders had chosen this temporary base in part because the British Museum Library was easily defendable from lupanoid attacks, with the Reading Room perched in the center of an interior open courtyard, and it had only endured minor damage in the Blitz. But they also chose it to remind the soldiers what they were fighting for, what life had once been like.

Sydney turned to a nearby soldier and raised his eyebrows in question, wondering about the man in the lupanoid cloak. The soldier shrugged and passed the same questioning look to another. Eventually, the question made it to Lieutenant Wyndham's cot on the edge of the officers' section. Wyndham puffed his cheeks with a resigned sigh and picked up a deck of cards. He walked over to Sydney's cot and sat on one end, checking first to ensure that the lupanoid-draped man was out of earshot. The young soldiers nearby circled their cots as if readying for a game of whist. Wyndham dealt cards to three of the closest men. Then he began. "Listen, brothers, to know the wrath of Alexander."

Just before these raging wolf-men made it into London, I came down here with Captain Ernest Harrell to recruit soldiers for the Confrontation. Alexander and Patrick were some of our first volunteers. They'd met, I think, during the war with Germany and seemed to prefer the military lifestyle to conventional London life.

Alexander had somehow heard about our strategy of tranq-ing the hell-dogs to avoid spilling their blood and attracting more. He came armed with an old elephant tranquilizer gun that his father had used in African safaris. A beautiful piece to be sure, and he had even named it Peleus, for some reason. Captain Harrell tried to insist that he use one of our regular tranqs, but Alexander refused. I think it was because of this that Harrell never seemed to trust him, and he was uneasy around both of them. I don't know.

Patrick was tall and strong with black hair and blue eyes that carried the confident look of a successful soldier. He wore a necklace with a ruby pendant shaped like a flame with a large "A" in the center. And likewise, Alexander wore an emerald pendant shaped like a four-leaf clover with a "P" in the center. Of course, we all saw what was going on. The older soldiers, the ones who had fought in the war, seemed to understand this and let it go unmentioned. Maybe they saw that kind of thing more often, I don't know. But many of us were frankly uncomfortable around it, especially being so open. We didn't antagonize, just kept our distance.

And it's true that Alexander and Patrick made a solid team, as soldiers, I mean. We all saw it when the lupes finally migrated to the city. Sometimes, Alexander would charge right into an area to rouse the devils, and Patrick would cover him at a distance. They shot true and without hesitation, landing each target with one well-placed dart, even with that old elephant gun. That's really why no one talked to them about their… relationship. They were the best warriors in the company.

I remember the ambush in Trafalgar Square, in particular. Captain Harrell had devised hiding places throughout the square for nearly our whole battalion, but we needed to somehow lure a large group of the beasts there without causing an uncontrollable feeding frenzy. Without hesitation, Alexander volunteered, and Patrick right behind him. They located a pack loitering under the trees of Leicester Square nearby. To make sure they'd be up for a chase, Patrick sliced his own hand and dripped the blood down Saint Martin's Street from Trafalgar to Leicester.

It worked. The devils were already sniffing the air when Alexander began yelling from one corner of the park. As a pack, they turned and ran toward him, growling and drooling and snarling. He and Patrick ran down Saint

Martin's over the trail of blood, even as Patrick was dripping more. Somehow they made it. They led the hell-dogs directly past the National Academy where we were waiting for them. I saw them dash from around a corner laughing and whooping like American Indians. Alexander had lost his hat, and his blond hair, shaggy even then, flowed freely, and he waved old Peleus over his head. And close on their heels was the most terrifying pack of foam-mouthed monsters you can imagine. I've not seen anything like it before or since, and I hope none of you ever do. But we took down every one of them, and our only casualty was Patrick's self-inflicted wound.

Almost every Confrontation soldier who was there that night was impressed by their bravery. We'd given slim odds of them outrunning a hungry pack with blood in its nostrils. But they did, and they seemed to love it. They embraced each other tightly after the last beast collapsed, and I thought Patrick must be feeling faint because of the way he buried his face into Alexander's neck and shoulder. I sent the medic over to tend to him as I helped the others drag the unconscious lupe bodies into the waiting trucks for transport to the crematorium.

A day or two later, I accompanied Captain Harrell to the desk that served as his office, over by the botany books, to retrieve some supply requests. On the far edge, where Alexander still sleeps today, we passed him and Patrick facing each other on two cots pulled rather close together. Alexander was carefully refreshing the bandage on Patrick's hand. I noticed for the first time then how delicate and tender he could be and the loving expression with which Patrick watched his friend's work.

Before I could comprehend what I was witnessing, though, Captain Harrell stomped over to them. He kicked Alexander's cot out from under him, and it slammed against the wall. Patrick stood, reaching for his friend on the ground. Harrell roared at him that the Confrontation had nurses to replace bandages and that he had better go see one before… well, he threatened a few actions that made Patrick blush and my mouth drop open in astonishment. Not things appropriate for a gentleman and an officer, even in anger. Without saying a word, Patrick lowered his eyes and hurried over to the medical camp in the courtyard, the tail of the untied bandage fluttering behind him.

Sydney could feel the heat in the face and knew it must be glowing, despite the chill in the room. He peeked over his shoulder and saw that the man, Alexander, had slung the lupe cloak over one cot and lay face up on the one next to it, as if claiming both. He draped his arm over his eyes, but Sydney noticed a bitter and sorrowful twist to the mouth. He recognized that look; he'd seen it in the glass of his own shaving kit.
Wyndham continued his story.

Alexander lifted himself slowly from the floor, eyes full of rage. Harrell ignored him, turned his back to him and waved me toward his office. Behind him, I saw Alexander rise up as if to strike him. I started to shout, but hesitated. And so did Alexander. I'm not sure why, but something made him catch himself. Instead, he picked up his bedding and righted his cot. I followed Harrell to the office.

When I went back to my own bed later, I noticed that Alexander was lying on his back slowly shaking his head. Patrick sat on his own cot, a little farther away now, and seemed to be pleading with Alexander.

I don't know what they finally agreed to. The next day, we readied for our regular morning sweep of Bloomsbury. Patrick came out into the courtyard alone carrying Peleus. Harrell asked him directly where Alexander was, but Patrick just shrugged. Harrell stormed into the Reading Room and left us waiting outside. Patrick stood stoically, not at full attention, but not comfortable either, and avoided our questioning looks. Harrell stomped out alone, just as angry as he had been when he went in, and slapped the rear of a pretty red-headed nurse who was standing near the medic camp in the courtyard. He ordered us to march without any explanation. But I fell in near him and heard him muttering about the cowardice necessary to eat the Confrontation's rations and sleep under the Confrontation's protection but refuse to fight.

The sweep was quieter than usual, and we took down only two of the demons—Patrick caught one of them with Peleus, which performed as well for him as for Alexander. We took our time with the sweep, not knowing what awaited us.

Upon returning here to the museum, we understood why it had been so quiet. There were several packs of beasts near the main entrance, battling with one another over some offal in the street. I assumed that the monsters had just happened to catch one of the few remaining dogs in the city and were fighting over it, but then I noticed that some of the meat was chained to the fence. It seemed that someone had killed and sliced open a lupanoid and hung it like a wreath on our front door.

We took positions around the street and began tranq-ing as many of the hell-dogs as we could, but there were so many of them, and they had been worked into a rage before we stumbled upon them. Since we'd just been conducting a routine patrol, we didn't have enough tranquilizer darts on hand to combat all of them. Several soldiers fell during the fight soon after running out of ammo.

Captain Harrell saw this and shouted that we would have to get into the courtyard to get more darts for the men. Patrick suddenly appeared next to me and shouted that he would go, but he needed cover. Harrell and I nodded and took up positions. Patrick took a deep breath, kissed Peleus's barrel, and sprinted toward the beasts blocking the entrance.

Sydney inhaled sharply when Wyndham suddenly turned and looked directly at him. He shoved the letter he'd been writing under his pillow. He opened his mouth to object, to defend himself, to renounce everything he could think of, but his breath caught in his parched throat. Wyndham turned away and threw a few cards down as if making a whist play. Sydney realized then that Wyndham been looking over him, checking on Alexander at the far side of the room. He released his breath but continued to feel his heart rapping in his throat.

Harrell and I did the best we could to keep the lupes off him. But there were too many. I saw the one that got him. Patrick saw it too. He raised the elephant gun and pulled the trigger, but nothing happened. The gun was jammed, and Patrick didn't know how to correct it or didn't have time. He grabbed it by the barrel and swung it like a club, fighting off two devils before the third one took him down. It stood on his bleeding, broken body and howled, raising its head and white-tufted tail in the air.

At the howl, the others paused in their attack and turned towards the fresh kill. The lupe with the white-tipped tail growled and circled Patrick's body. Others snarled in return. One lunged at the killer, then another knocked it off balance, and soon the monsters were tearing at Patrick, pulling his body in opposite directions.

Harrell's eyes widened with ire and fear. He screamed at us to advance, so we did. Those who had run out of darts fought with their knives or swung their guns as Patrick had. It was a weak offense, and we suffered for it. Harrell was bitten in the neck, and his blood showered over us. We continued to fight, though, and eventually it was enough. We were able to retreat into the old bookstore across Great Russell Street, dragging what was left of our brothers, Patrick, Harrell, and the others. The hell-dogs still blocked the entrance to the museum, and we had no choice but to wait them out.

After several hours of snapping at one another over the few scraps of meat that the tranq-ed and slain fiends provided, the beasts finished all they could and cleared out of the street, retreating to what horrible place we knew not what. I crept out to survey the museum entrance and gave the safety signal to the lookout in the bookstore window.

I entered the courtyard as the bookstore door creaked open and soldiers emerged bearing broken bodies. The medics and nurses, who had been pinned in by the fighting, rushed towards me, dabbing at some scrapes and the blood covering my clothes, but I waved them on to the others.

I went straight for the Reading Room and opened the door. The room was empty of humans, save Alexander. I saw him sitting cross-legged and cross-armed on his cot, scowling. Two fully packed duffle bags sat next to him on Patrick's cot. When he saw me enter, he jumped up and seized the bags. "He understands now, doesn't he?" he asked, voice low but shaking in anger. "Harrell, the hypocrite, knows how much he needs me fighting alongside him. I will not stay here and be disgraced by such as him!"

Alexander advanced toward the door with the two bags, one marked with an A and the other with a P. I could hear the others arriving in the courtyard with the dead. But I couldn't find the words to warn him.

As soon as he laid eyes on Patrick's mangled body, he collapsed onto his knees. He wailed to the open sky, a nearly inhuman moan, not dissimilar to the lupe that had howled over its kill. He crawled to Patrick's torn body and buried his face in his blood-soaked chest. He wept, heavily and for a long time. He didn't even look up when Harrell's body was placed near him.

Sydney thought of his friend, who might be in Australia already. He cleared his throat and frowned, the most masculine way he knew to smother an onset of tears. Wyndham absent-mindedly collected the cards he had thrown. He added them to the deck and shuffled in twice. When he spoke again, his eyes fixed on a sky blue panel of the dome above their heads.

Now that Harrell was dead, I was the senior officer until a replacement arrived. I waved the men away from this spectacle of grief, and we ate a grim supper together. When I returned later, I found Alexander lying alongside Patrick's body. After glancing at the darkening sky, I asked some nearby men to construct a pyre in the courtyard. We would burn the bodies here, tonight, and avoid attracting any more monsters.

As they began their work, I rested my hand on Alexander's shoulder.

"He fought so bravely," I told him. "He was trying to get a resupply of tranqs when they fell upon him. He fought off two, but the third, with a white-tipped tail, got him."

Alexander sobbed loudly and turned away.

As soon as the pyre was ready in the dim light of late evening, we loaded Harrell and the other soldiers onto it. No one cried for them in the same way, although several did cry. Once the fire roared around their bodies, I turned to tell Alexander that it was time. But Patrick lay on the ground alone. As I looked around to see where Alexander could have gone, the courtyard gate slammed open as if kicked, and Alexander stood massively on the threshold. His face was lit by the fire, but the flames within his eyes smoldered deeper. He walked heavily into the courtyard dragging two lupes by their tails. They were unconscious but alive.

He dropped them near the pyre. No one said a word as he turned towards Patrick's body and knelt beside it. He stroked Patrick's head and muttered something. He then gently slid the belt from around Patrick's waist and the necklace from around his neck, setting them to the side. Lifting the body over his shoulder, he carried it over to the pyre and tossed it in. With tears streaming from his eyes, then, he lifted the head of one of the hell-dogs by grabbing the fur between its ears. He pulled the knife from his belt, raised his red eyes to the starry night, and slit the beast's throat. It gurgled and choked, and blood spewed onto the pyre.

The men yelled and jumped back, and I signaled to them that they should not interfere. Alexander kicked the lupe body to the bottom of the pyre and methodically repeated this ritual with the other unconscious beast. He knelt on the ground and pulled at his hair, yelling to the flames and the sparks shooting into the night that he would have his revenge. The smell of burning flesh filled our nostrils and clothes. Most of us wandered away, ashamed.

The next morning, Alexander's bed had not been slept in. Instead of looking for him, though, I thought it best to give him some time to pull himself together. We went on our regular morning patrol, heading northeast.

We'd only made it to Russell Square when we saw him. He looked humped and monstrous from afar, and I signaled the men to take offensive positions. As he drew closer, I saw that Alexander had a lupe slung over his shoulders, like a woman's shawl. He walked slowly but steadily under its weight, his face a chiseled mask of anger. The men began whispering and lowered their weapons. As he passed through the group without looking at or acknowledging us, we saw that he was drenched in blood and stunk of lupanoid. And the creature over his shoulders had a white-tipped tail.

I let him go. He seemed to be in another world, and shocking him back to ours might have been dangerous.

But we followed the bloody trail that he left behind him, which led us to the old Russell Square tube station. The door, which was boarded up last I'd seen, had been bashed and hung loose on its hinges. I swung it open with the barrel of my tranq and was greeted with a foul odor—too much life mingled with recent death.

The men followed me in hesitantly. A few of them had remembered to bring their torches, and we looked around.

I've used the word *massacre* prior to this, but it would take a lot for me to use it again. It seemed clear that the devils had been living in the bowels of London for some time without our knowledge. The place was littered with ripped paper and stuffing, picked-clean bones, and reeking waste. But instead of a den, we entered a morgue. Their wretched bodies were scattered down the stairs, across the platform, and along the tracks. Blood dripped steadily from nearly every ledge. Each drop was quiet, but there were so many, so much blood, such a hot stink, I felt deafened and suffocated.

We examined a few of the lupes and found that most of them had been sliced or stabbed. A few others seemed simply crushed or beaten. It's rare that we even severely injure one of these brutes before cremation, so this sight was all the more shocking. Under one of them, I found Peleus, broken in several places. And hanging from the top end of the stair railing was Patrick's necklace with the ruby flame. When the men began vomiting, I pulled us out of there.

Later that day, after the new commanding officer arrived, a few of us returned and drenched the platform and tracks with fuel, as far into the tubes as we dared. We set fire to the Underground and left, securing the door behind us.

As far as I know, it's still burning down there.

Lieutenant Wyndham fell silent then. Sydney glanced over at Alexander, who remained motionless on his cot, still scowling with his eyes covered. He then looked at the expressions on the faces of his brothers in arms who had heard the story. Some quietly watched the lieutenant, waiting for more closure. Others grimaced and nudged each other with giggles. Sydney made eye contact with one of the men, someone he hadn't met yet, who looked shaken. He had an impulse to squeeze his hand.

Wyndham collected the cards that the men still clutched, un-played. He kept his eyes lowered and cleared his throat. "He's worn that skin ever since. He keeps fighting the hell-dogs, as strongly as ever, but he doesn't enjoy it like he used to. And he's more… brutal." Wyndham stood then, nodded, and walked back to his own cot.

The little group broke up, each retreating to his own space. Sydney pulled the letter from under his pillow. The words he saw were full of sorrow, fear, and recrimination. He crumpled it as quietly as he could and stuffed it under his thin mattress. Then he pulled out a clean sheet of paper and began again.

Admiral October

Levi Hastings

OBLIVIOUS IMPERIALISM IS THE WORST KIND
CAConrad

is ho-bo
short for
something
i just got
called one
someone
recently said
"HEY your nails
are beautiful but
the rest of your
outfit is just ok"
glamor is my
great love but is
too expensive and
too much work
my beautiful
glittered nails are
my HOMAGE to GLAMOR
every time i hear an interview
with a fashion model talking
about HOW HARD her job is
walking up and down the runway
up and down
so much walking
i become very tired in my
vicarious glamor fatigue
and i must nap
everyone around
the world knows
america's real
fashion statement
is bullet holes
every single

day we
spray the arab world
with bullets
sometimes in
the faces of
babies we
don't have
special
little
bullets
for the
baby
faces they
have to take
our adult sized
bullets right in
the middle of
their little
crying baby
faces BLAM take
THAT BABY it's
american
fashion

Zombie Autopsy
for anelosimus octavius

Janie Miller

Wasp eggs in my lung grow a body on a petri dish,
five bodies, a virus.
God's dialogue of apples forgot the plague,
and homo sapiens.
Part the lung's curtain further to a woman's hand,
alabaster, window model.
We model when the moon is on top of us, bodies
flailing in space
away from ocean. Our mother's salty milk
told us who to be
until sex took over, but her hand held—
puppet strings, sagging accordion.
My body a curio cabinet of history. This verse
ladled in larval stew.
Viral wasp gestures through the window
for its brood.

Quota

⚙

Amy Shepherd

I FINISHED OFF my watery G & T and signaled to the bartender for another, flicking my ash onto the floor. The thin wail of the performer cut through the pulsing music and drunken laughter.

This back room of a Chinese restaurant was different from the bars I typically frequented for work. Whether low-rent with sawdust on the floor or high-priced with cocaine flowing like wine, they were places where desperation hung stagnant as the air in a privy.

Here, the air smelled of greasy Chinese food, but there was a buzz—the anticipation of performance, the giddiness of release through song. Still, with my job, I was never really off the clock, and my attention was drawn like maggot to wound by one lone unhappy girl. I ground out my cigarette underneath my boot and made my way to her past a stockpile of broken, rusty chairs.

"Not going to sing tonight?" I asked, lighting a new cigarette and nodding towards the makeshift stage with its weak red lighting. A song list binder was spread out on the table, her hand half-covering the Madonna section.

She shook her head. "Too chickenshit." She was still in her work drag, a cut-rate poly-cotton blend navy blue pantsuit, with her pumps kicked off underneath the rickety table.

"There's joy in giving yourself over to music," I said.

She shook her head, not agreeing or perhaps not hearing me over the clash of a Metallica number starting.

I gently moved her hand so I could view the list. "Which one would you like to sing?" I asked.

She pulled the binder closer to her and bent in the dim light. She scanned the list, flipping page after page. If not Madonna, then I would guess for her Alanis Morissette. She surprised me by picking "House of the Rising Sun."

"No way could I pull it off though. ABBA's more my speed," she said, pushing the binder away and circling her glass in the condensation on the table.

"Want another?" I asked, tapping the rim of her glass with my finger.

She squinted at me in the low light. I stood still for a long moment, letting her assess me, her gaze sliding down my body, from my long blond hair to my quick-bitten fingernails to my Doc Martens.

"OK. Vodka cranberry."

When I returned with fresh drinks, I saw that she'd moved all the empties down to one end of the table, clearing a spot for us. Napkins lay in a sodden pile near the glasses.

I set her drink in front of her, then took a seat. "My name is Ruth," I said, offering her my hand.

Her grip was firm, all her fingers engaged. "My name is Jennifer, like everyone else here." She pointed across the room to a far table. "Jennifer K, currently sleeping with her boss. Jennifer M, dad owns the firm. Jennifer A, prefers to be called Jenny."

"It's a work party? Why aren't you over there with them?" I asked, leaning in closer.

She laughed. "It was a pity invite. I don't know why I even came."

"Where do you work?" I lit a cigarette, blew the smoke away from us.

"Ad agency. I'm as good as fired though," she said and drained her glass. I hadn't noticed until now that it bore lip marks in a shade of lipstick not her own.

"Why?" I asked, suppressing the urge to tuck a loose strand of her hair behind her ear. Her face was flushed from the alcohol.

"'Cause I'm a failure at everything I do," she said. The lack of emotion in her voice surprised me.

I touched her lightly on the forearm. "I'll do a song with you. You pick, I'll sing. I've got a good voice."

Now I was surprising myself. I never participated in human social customs anymore, just haunted the margins. But I had once loved to sing. In fact, I was prideful about my voice. As the elders used to say, pride goeth before the fall.

She had a skeptical look on her face. I didn't wait for her assent though, just squeezed her arm and got up. "We need a couple more drinks first. You stay here, pick a song."

By the time I got back, she'd have a song picked out and have started to sing it under her breath. People had a tendency to agree with my suggestions.

Jennifer surprised me again by picking "Jackson" by June and Johnny Cash. I submitted our names to the DJ, and we plowed through two more drinks, which I was careful to have poured into clean glasses. As we walked to the stage, Jennifer was weaving a bit. She had stripped off her jacket, and her lower back was damp where I'd slung my arm around her to help her up the steps to the stage.

I'd never before had an audience for my singing. Mostly, I'd sung in the barn or while doing chores. Being on-stage was surreal, lights swirling the smoke, a blur of faces, music shaking the speakers. I could understand better now why some of our clients chose musical careers.

We got off to a slow start on the fast-paced song, but were soon caught up in the rhythm. I'd expected Jennifer to hang back, but instead she stood dangerously close to the edge of the wobbly stage, holding the mike in her hand. She belted out the lyrics, shimmying and swinging her free arm in a lassoing motion. After we were done, she seemed reluctant to leave the stage.

She slumped hotly against me, grinning like a Cheshire cat and accepting the accolades of the Jennifers as we wove our way back to the table. I dumped her in her chair and went to the bar to get her a glass of water.

"That was fun as hell!" she yelled and gulped water. "Let's do another one!"

As ever, I was amazed by alcohol's mood-altering effects. I never got so much as tipsy now, and, of course, I'd never tasted alcohol when I was human.

I didn't resist the temptation to push her hair back behind her ear this time. As my fingers grazed her face, she looked over at me, and for a second, I saw Rachel, her youth, her innocence. I pulled my hand away, and Jennifer frowned.

She reached out and took my hand. "What's wrong?"

"Nothing. You just remind me of someone I used to know." I turned away and took a big gulp from my drink, willing it for once to have a soothing effect.

Her hand moved to my back, and I felt her breath hot against my ear. "You remind me of someone too."

I watched as she slid a cigarette from my pack, lit it coughingly. She thrust it toward me, and I snatched it as it moved perilously close to my hair. My hair, another damning vanity.

"Let's do another song," I said, standing up.

She picked Tori Amos's "Silent All these Years," which I didn't know, but I caught on enough to sing the chorus. It was a quiet song, lost in the din of the bar. Perhaps only I heard how beautifully Jennifer sang it or saw the wet trails of tears on her face.

After the song, I took her home. She said little on the way, and I could feel the exhaustion pour off her. I walked with her through the brightly lighted corridors of her apartment building, forced her to drink a glass of water, and put her to bed.

I don't know why I didn't leave. I sat smoking in her bedroom, watching over her like I was a guardian angel instead of the one who would claim her soul. When dawn cast the sky pink, I twitched aside the curtains and watched the sun beginning to rise. In almost two centuries, I had rarely missed a sunrise.

I left my calling card on her kitchen table and pulled the door locked behind me. On the stoop of her apartment building, I lit a cigarette and watched the sun fill the sky.

Jennifer's call came much later in the day, when the winter sun had almost set.

"Thanks for taking me home last night. I was pretty drunk. I had a wicked hangover all day today."

"You're welcome. You sang beautifully. Why were you afraid to do it?"

"I don't know, afraid of making a fool of myself, I guess. I don't really go out much. The Jennifers kind of roped me into it. They feel sorry for me. When they're not resenting me anyway. My mom kind of got me the job. She knows the owner."

"You said yesterday you'd been fired."

"No, not fired. Just given an impossible assignment which will likely lead to me being fired."

"What is it? Maybe I can help."

"Make bran sexy."

"Pardon me?"

"That's my assignment. My boss said, 'Jennifer, make bran sexy.' Asshole. He thinks he's funny."

"What does bran have to do with anything?"

"Oh, the campaign's for Colon Health Month. One of the local hospitals wants to do a PSA on the benefits of fiber."

"I don't know much about marketing."

"There's not much to know. We convince people to buy shit they don't need. And to do that, we tap into base instincts: sex, greed, envy."

"Not your dream job then?"

"Hell, no. I studied journalism in college, thought I'd be a big-time news reporter. I can't get a job in that field now though."

"Why not?"

"Because I fucked up," Jennifer said and paused. "What about you, Ruth? What do you do?"

"I'm in sales."

"Then you know what I'm talking about, trying to sell people stuff they don't need."

"Actually, people are desperate for what I sell."

"OK, I'll bite. What do you sell?"

Now it was my turn to hedge. "I'd rather not talk about it over the phone."

"Now my interest is piqued. Is it drugs? Marital aids? Are you a loan shark?"

I laughed. "I guess you'll have to wait and see."

We made a date to meet up for coffee after work later in the week.

She was dressed more casually this time, in jeans and a puffy blue down jacket, a gray and red striped scarf wrapped around her neck. Her face was ruddy from the cold and dark brown hair spilled over her collar. She brightened when she saw me.

"I wasn't sure I'd remember you, to be honest. I was that drunk. But you have a striking face," she said as we slipped into line.

"It's my Scandinavian heritage. We were all tall, blue-eyed blonds in my family."

"Yeah? I'm a European mutt, a little of everything, English, German, Italian."

We had gotten our drinks and moved towards a table when she touched my arm.

"Do you want to go outside and walk instead?"

I agreed, tightening my scarf and pulling out my gloves.

"I can't believe you like green tea. It's so bitter," said Jennifer.

"Life is bitter."

"You're kind of odd, aren't you? That's cool, I like it."

Sorting through my emotions, I wasn't sure what to say. Jennifer felt like a kindred spirit, but it wasn't smart to get involved with a potential client. Nevertheless, I said, "I like you too, Jennifer."

We walked the frosty sidewalks in silence and then turned into a park. It looked like the kind of place where grandmothers got robbed of their rolls of nickels. We walked past a tarp-covered mound of dirt to a splintery-looking bench tucked away in the shadow of an anemic lamppost.

"I used to come here when I was a kid. Sometimes I can't believe I live in the same neighborhood I grew up in. I went away to college, to Columbia. I never thought I'd come back here."

"Chicago's not so bad."

Jennifer sat on the bench, her gloved hands huddling her cup. "No, it's fine. It's just, I thought I'd be, I don't know, traveling the world in search of Pulitzer-winning stories about third-world orphans or something."

"Have you tried to get a job at a paper here? Maybe I could help."

"Nope, once they checked my references, it'd be all over. Let's talk about something else, OK?"

I knew I should probe deeper into her story, maybe even make the offer, but I found myself unable to do it. I told myself I didn't want to rush things, but the truth was, I'd never let a transaction drag out this long before.

I tossed my cup onto an overflowing trash barrel and took up a perch on the top of the bench, lighting a cigarette. "I grew up in southern Illinois on a farm. Green fields, rolling hills, God's country."

"What was it like growing up on a farm?"

My mind drifted to visions of the barn, the rope thrown over the rafter, Rachel's legs dangling, her boots carefully lined up on the ground.

I was aware of taking too long to answer, Jennifer's eyes on me. "Lonely," I said finally, flicking my cigarette away and stepping off the bench. I pulled on my gloves. "We should get going."

Jennifer stood. She took off her glove and stowed it in a jacket pocket, then peeled off my glove and stuffed it in my pocket. She laced her cold, dry fingers through mine.

She is really nothing like Rachel, I thought as she kissed me.

I'd seen Jennifer almost every day for two weeks, and I had yet to make the offer, despite hearing numerous blow-by-blows from her miserable work life. I'd signed few other contracts, so the summons to see my boss was not unexpected.

I sat across from him, dwarfed by the enormous slab of redwood he used for a desk. Rumor had it, he felled the tree himself with one blow of the axe. I swirled the scotch in its snifter like he had taught me. I took a sniff, then a mouthful. The liquid was smoky on my tongue. I could practically taste the peat.

"Laphroaig?" I asked.

"Pfft. Longrow, 10 years aged. You drink too much cheap liquor. It dulls the tongue." He dropped his cuff links to the desk and rolled up his sleeves.

"Ordering single malt scotch in some of the bars I frequent would be like waving a red flag in a bull's face. You want me to get mugged?"

"One thing I know about you, Ruth, is that you can take care of yourself." He came around to my side of the desk, propped one meaty thigh on it, and put his hand on my shoulder. "Now what's wrong, kiddo? You're way below quota this month. And the contracts you have signed, well, not your finest work."

He ticked the contracts off on his fingers. "A mother who wants guaranteed beauty pageant wins for her ugly daughter, a man who desires to become irresistible to women, but only blond ones, and a man who wishes to bind his wife to him even though she loves another. There are more things in heaven and earth, Ruth."

"I know, I'm sorry. I've been distracted," I said, sliding my glass onto his desk and tucking my hands under my thighs. "I think I'm falling in love with one of my clients."

"Have you made the offer yet?"

"No."

"But you want to."

"Yes. I want to help her."

He snorted, slapped his thigh. "Ah, Ruth, you are precious. Such a Pollyanna."

"You know that's the only way I can do this job. To think of it as helping them. I can't take joy in it. I'm not a bad person."

"Nor are you good. You forget, Ruth, I have known you your whole life, through all your perversions." He stood and stretched, then patted my shoulder. "I'm not criticizing you, my dear. Far from it. Year after year, you exceed our quotas."

"What should I do?" I scuffed the toe of my boot into the ivory pile rug.

He stroked his goatee. "Have you lain with her?"

"No," I said, looking at the floor.

"Lay with her. Get it out of your system. Then you'll be able to sign her."

Afterwards, I felt like I'd exhaled for the first time in about a decade. I sat on the edge of the bed naked, stroking her silken thigh and smoking a cigarette.

"Why do you smoke so much?" she asked, holding out her hand for my cigarette. She took a puff and coughed.

"I think it's safe to say that smoking's not your thing," I said, taking it back from her.

"You look so sexy, I wanted to try it."

I smiled. "Stay here, I have a gift for you."

I came back, holding a bottle of Laphroaig and two glasses. "You didn't have any ice. We'll have to drink it straight." I poured us each a scotch.

Jennifer took a swig and made a face. "Yuck. It tastes like smoke. Is that why you like it?"

"Try another sip. It's an acquired taste."

"When have you had time to acquire all these tastes anyway?"

"I'm older than I look."

"How much older? 30?"

I laughed. "I've never told you what I do for a living, so to speak."

"No, you haven't. Now your age is a mystery too. You're my mystery woman."

I walked to the bathroom and ran water over the cigarette butt to extinguish it, then placed it in the waste can. I slipped back into bed, and Jennifer rolled onto her side, turning away from me. I lifted her hair and kissed the nape of her neck, then kissed my way down her back, savoring each knobby vertebra.

She rolled back to face me and pulled my chin up to hers. She kissed my brow. "Your eyes are so sad. I never knew blue eyes could be sad."

I tried to stay in the moment, but my mind kept flying back to Rachel, that day by the river, the sun shining on her bare breasts, bits of grass entangled in her hair, her mouth an O of pleasure.

"Whoever she was, forget her. You're with me now." She pushed me onto my back, straddled me, took my breasts in her hands. She leaned over and kissed me, kissed me, kissed me.

I snagged a pea pod from Jennifer's plate with my chopsticks and placed it in my mouth. It tasted like wet cardboard. I had no appetite. The clock was ticking away and still no contract.

I'd taken my boss's advice, quite a few times as a matter of fact. But I was still no closer to sealing the deal. Tonight was the night, I decided, and out of respect for Jennifer, I was determined to do it without using my power to convince her.

"You're so good with those chopsticks. Is that another of your acquired tastes?" she asked, forking through the uneaten food on my plate. She found a squiggle of chicken and speared it.

I shrugged, setting down my chopsticks and pushing my plate towards her.

"Why are you so quiet this evening?" she asked, taking my hand.

"We need to talk," I said, pulling my hand away and reaching for my pack of cigarettes.

Jennifer stiffened. "Are you breaking up with me?"

"No, of course not." I laid aside my unlit cigarette and took her hand. "Why would you think that?"

"In my experience, 'we need to talk' usually translates to 'Jennifer, I'm going to dump your ass.'"

"Sweetheart." I reached out and stroked her cheek. "When I first saw you in that bar, I was drawn to you. I felt a very strong connection. I still do."

"Oh yeah? What'd you first notice about me?" she asked with a smile, at once shy and flirtatious.

"Your pain. It called out to me."

Jennifer twisted her head away and leaned back in her seat, crossing her arms over her chest. "My pain? I know I'm a bit of a glass-half-empty gal, but still, that's harsh, saying the first thing you noticed about me was my pain."

"I'm saying this all wrong." I leaned forward and smoothed her hair. "You're beautiful, Jennifer, even in your sadness. I saw the way you were sitting alone, and it made me want to help you."

Jennifer got up. "Thanks, I guess."

"I know what it's like to be lonely, to be sad. You don't have to face it alone."

She crossed her arms again and frowned. "This is starting to sound like a PSA, Ruth. I thought you were in sales. Are you secretly a therapist or something?"

"I'm not a therapist. But I do help people."

"Help them how?"

"Jennifer, do you trust me?"

"Well, I did, before you asked me that. Now I'm not so sure. Why are you being so mysterious about your job?" She started clearing the table, keeping an eye on me like she was afraid I'd make off with her silverware.

I sat forward, erect in my chair. "It's hard to explain. I need you to trust me."

She started running water into the sink. "Tell you what. You tell me what you do, and then I'll trust you, OK?"

"I help people…"

She swiveled her head. "So you've said. How do you help them?" she asked, over-enunciating the words.

I needed to regain control of this conversation. I could see the contract slipping away from me. I walked over to her, hovered by her elbow, and spoke quietly. "I want this to be your choice, Jennifer. I haven't influenced you so far because I want it to be right for you. But I know I can help you if you'd only let me."

She turned off the faucet and gripped the edge of the sink, carefully not looking at me. "I don't like where this is going. You make it sound as if I may not have a choice… in something, but you won't say what it is. You need to tell me right now what you're talking about or this conversation is over."

I blew out a breath. "I sell success, Jennifer. Happiness. Whatever a person wants. In exchange for his or her soul."

She turned and looked at me, dumbfounded. "Their soul?"

"Yes, their soul."

"And you want to help me," she said slowly, her forehead pinched in thought.

"Yes, whatever would make you happy, I can give it to you."

"In exchange for my soul."

"Yes." I smiled, feeling my confidence return.

Jennifer shook her head and rubbed the back of her neck as if it were suddenly sore. "Well, that's just about the craziest thing I've ever heard. I don't even know what to say."

"Say yes. Let me help you." I took both her hands in mine.

She pulled out of my grip and grabbed the dishtowel. "No offense, Ruth, but you're the one who needs help, not me."

Jennifer looked at me for a long moment, the same sadness that had drawn us together now pushing us apart. She turned her back to me, wiped her hands on the towel. "It's late. I think you should go."

I turned her around to face me. I feared that I had lost her. I didn't want to lose the contract too. "I know you don't believe me, but it's true. I work for the Devil. I grant people's wildest dreams, and they give me their souls in return."

She touched my face. "Baby, don't do this. Go home, OK? Call me tomorrow. Maybe we can pretend this never happened."

I gripped her wrist in my hand. "I need you to believe me. I can still help you."

Annoyance flickered across her face, chased by doubt and a touch of fear. She spoke slowly as if to a wayward child. "Ruth, let go of me."

"Not until you say yes," I said.

"Let go of me now. Go home before you do something we both regret."

I tightened my grip.

"Goddamn it, Ruth. I know self-defense. Don't make me kick your ass."

She yanked her arm, trying to get free, but I was a dog with a bone. Why had I thought I could do this without using my power?

"Don't say I didn't warn you," she said and stomped on my foot. I lost my hold on her, and she crossed the kitchen in three strides, putting the table between us. She started rooting around in her handbag.

I covered the distance just as quickly, leaned across the table towards her. "I'll prove it to you. I know things about you no one else knows."

"Ruth, I'm begging you. Go the fuck home. Don't make me call the police." She held up her cell phone.

"When you were eight, you stole a candy bar from the market, an Almond Joy. That's how you discovered that you hated coconut, but you ate the whole thing anyway."

"That's it, I'm dialing. You have about 30 seconds."

I plucked the phone out of her hand, threw it behind me. "That same year, you found a pornographic magazine in your friend's garage. You touched yourself for the first time, then hid it under a pile of greasy rags. Next time you went to his house, you looked for the magazine, but it was gone."

I could see she was shocked, but whether at my words or my actions, I didn't know. I was shocked myself. This had gone so very wrong. But I'd come too far to leave empty-handed now.

She shoved the table towards me, forcing me to back up.

"That car wreck— you didn't hit a post like you told your dad. You killed the neighbor's dog, just left it lying in the ditch and rushed home to wash off the blood before your dad saw it."

"Please, stop." Her face was painted with shame, sorrow. My heart fisted in my chest.

"The man who raped you in college—you knew him. You had kissed him before, maybe even teased him. You thought it was your fault."

She was hanging on the table now, softening into the floor, her face ruined by tears.

"Jennifer, I can make it all better. Just let me help you."

I skirted the table to stand over her and reached out a hand. She shrank from me. I stood watching her as my power gathered, throbbed in my fingertips. Time ticked by in slow motion. I felt the heat rising off her head, only inches away from my hand's caress.

Curling fingers into palm, I withdrew my hand. I picked my things up off the floor and left.

"Did you lay with her?" He was lounging in his chair, his head wreathed in cigar smoke.

I waved smoke away from my face. "Yes."

"Did you make the offer?"

"Yes."

"Unsuccessful?"

I leaned my elbows on the desk, held my head in my hands. "Yes."

He leaned forward, his red face emerging luminous through the smoke. "Forget about her then. What is it they say? When God closes a door, he opens a window." He threw back his head with laughter, giving me a glimpse of his many gold fillings.

"I can't forget."

"Then use your power to have her." He set his cigar in an ornate crystal ashtray and turned his intense gaze on me.

"No, it's no good like that. It turns out badly." I slumped back into my seat.

"Ah, you are thinking of the first one, the one you gave your soul to have." He propped his chin on steepled hands and made a show of being thoughtful, like he was auditioning for the role of TV psychiatrist. "I have often wondered, Ruth. Was it worth it?"

"Yes."

He took up his cigar and reclined back into his chair as a smile spread across his face.

I shredded her file. I moved onto other contracts, signing marks in a frenzy of productivity. When she called the first time, I didn't pick up, nor the second. The third time though, I answered.

"I am so sorry, Jennifer," I said.

"I want to know. What can I get for selling my soul?"

"It's not your fault. You did nothing to deserve that." I wasn't sure if I was talking about the rape or the way I had acted last time I saw her.

"Are you listening to me? I said, I want to sell my soul."

"Jennifer, you don't have to do this. You have your whole life ahead of you. Things will work out, just give it time."

"Don't tell me what to do."

"I was wrong to think that's what you needed. I was wrong to ask that of you."

"Are you going to buy it or not? Do I have to find someone else to do your dirty work? Stand on a seedy street corner and wait for some other devil to walk by?"

I couldn't think of anything to say. There was nothing I wanted less than to do her contract.

"Well?"

"All right, Jennifer, if that's what you want, I can draw up a contract."

"You bet that's what I want. Why the hell else would I call you?"

"What will you take in exchange? Wealth, fame, love?"

"I sure as hell don't want love. I want to be a journalist. I want to write important stories, stories that matter."

"Success in career. Consider it done."

We set a date to meet the following week at Starbucks. I got there early, bought a jasmine green tea and a mocha for Jennifer. I'd never thought of Starbucks as a place to linger and was surprised to see nearly all the tables full, occupied by a single person each.

As I sat at my single-serving-size table, I felt pinpricks of longing, despair, and boredom scattered around the room like constellations in the night sky. Faces cast ghostly by the reflection of laptop screens, drinks forgotten and cooling. Donne was wrong; each person was an island, entire of itself.

Only one person sat, hands idle, an older gay gentleman cloaked in a trenchcoat. I followed the line of his gaze to the sole male working the counter. Likely, he'd been coming in for days now, ordering ever more complicated drinks, trying to catch the barista's eye.

The door clanged, and I swiveled my head, expecting Jennifer. Instead, a woman and her teenage daughter stalked in and took their place in line. Their bodies were etched with their fights, past, present, and future, ratcheting tight the muscles of their faces, their backs.

I could imagine the mother coming to me, years from now, wanting her youth back, her unlined face, her sense of an untainted world. The daughter would come too, seeking a release she had found only once on her own, the time she had held razor blade to wrist.

Clearly, I would have to rethink my night owl existence, working the bars. There was considerable business to be done here in the daylight, if I could stand it. The dull ache of human need without the surreality of the wee hours depressed even me.

I was swirling the last cold inch of my tea when Jennifer arrived. She stood in front of my table and squared her rain-darkened shoulders.

"I was starting to think you weren't coming," I said and gestured for her to sit.

She remained standing, her gaze fixed on the wall behind me.

"I bought you a mocha. One percent milk, right?"

Her eyes shifted to my face for a long, hateful look, and for a moment, I thought she might dash the mocha to the floor.

"Let's get this over with."

"Is there nothing I can say to change your mind?"

"No."

"Then we need somewhere private. You have to sign in blood."

"Bathroom," she said and started walking.

I threw our cups in the trash and walked down the dim hallway to where she was waiting, door propped open with her boot.

I stepped in, and she locked the door. I pulled down the baby-changing table and took a long, slender case out of my bag. My boss insisted on using the most modern encrypted e-sign technology, but I didn't want to go the computer route for this contract. The least I could do was to give Jennifer a memorable experience.

The exquisite signing kit had been given to me the first time I had exceeded my quota, more than a century and a half earlier. I lifted the brass inkwell out of its velvet cavity and unfolded the tortoiseshell lancet. Remembering her fingers inside me, I reached for her left hand. I squeezed her index finger until the tip turned purple, then raised the lancet.

"Wait," Jennifer said.

I let up on the pressure but continued to hold her finger, laying aside the lancet. I let out a breath I wasn't aware I'd been holding. It was a relief not to have to go through with this.

"Is that thing clean? I don't want to sell my soul just to end up with some disease."

I closed my eyes and tried to collect myself. "Yes, I sanitized it with bleach. There's no risk of infection."

"OK, then, get on with it."

Tightening my grip, I lanced her finger and squeezed the drops of blood into the inkwell. After I'd gathered enough, I pressed a cotton ball to the cut and handed her a Band-Aid.

"Have you ever done calligraphy?" I asked, readying the swan quill I'd made for her.

"Yes," she said, fussing with her Band-Aid.

"Well, it's like that. You don't have to press down very hard." I pulled out a small notebook. "Here, do a couple practice signatures."

"No, I'm ready now."

I looked at her, and her eyes defiantly met mine. There was fear, but also determination and pride. It made me wish I still had my soul to squander.

I unfurled her contract, a hand-lettered calfskin vellum scroll. I tucked the top under the case, and held the bottom flat with my hand. Without reading it, she signed the contract stating that she willingly gave over her soul to the Devil upon her death in exchange for success in her chosen career.

"Done," I said, holding out my hand for her to shake. It wasn't necessary to shake on the deal, but I couldn't bear the thought of never touching her again.

She shook, holding my hand like it was a dirty tissue, then left the bathroom. I gathered up my things and followed her, but she was gone before I could say goodbye.

About a year later, I began to see her byline pop up on the news sites. I didn't know if her stories were important. And I didn't know if anything could make a difference in this world. But it was a start.

One day, she called me out of the blue. I could hardly hear her over the background noise.

"I'm in Iraq. I'm doing a story on female soldiers."

"It's good to hear your voice, Jennifer. I'm sorry about everything."

"Well, I got what I wanted, thanks to you."

"Don't thank me. You did this all on your own. I never filed the paperwork."

"What do you mean? I signed a contract, in blood for God's sake."

"Never entered into the system. Never will be either. I burned it."

I remembered coming home from Starbucks that day, lighting a cigarette and settling in to re-read the contract, even though it was standard language, even though I knew it by heart. I must have read it ten times over, trying to decide what to do. Finally, I lit a match and touched it to the corner.

"Are you fucking with me? You better not be, not after everything you did."

"No, Jennifer, it's the truth."

"You weren't going to tell me, were you?"

"I don't know. I'm telling you now."

She shot a long sigh down the line. "Fuck, Ruth. I don't know whether to believe anything you say."

"I never lied to you, Jennifer."

"Well, you didn't exactly always tell the truth, did you?"

I said nothing. Over the last year, I had rehearsed countless times what I would say to Jennifer, given the chance. All of it, useless. After nearly 200 years, I still had no idea what to say to a woman I loved.

"Ruth, are you still there?"

"Yes."

"Thought I'd lost you. Phone service here sucks." Another pause as Jennifer coughed. "I guess I can't really get on your case about lying. I've done my share too. Did I ever tell you why I quit journalism to begin with?"

"No, you never told me." But I knew.

"When I was in college, I wrote a story on date rape. It won an award. It was my story, but I didn't want anyone to know so I changed a bunch of the details."

"That doesn't sound so bad."

"Well, in journalism, it's the equivalent of lying. They took my award away. My reputation was ruined. That killed what little self-respect I had left. I quit school, moved back in with my parents." She stopped, and I thought I heard a helicopter in the background.

I knew she didn't want to hear another "I'm sorry," especially from me, so I held my tongue.

"Anyway, Ruth, the reason I called is that I wanted to tell you that I forgive you. I know in your own fucked up way, you were trying to help."

"Thank you."

"I've got to go, OK? But promise me you'll try to forgive yourself."

"Take care, Jennifer. It was good talking to you."

I set the phone down and lit a cigarette, watching the waning light through the window. After I'd smoked it down to the filter, I got back to work. I had quotas to exceed.

Demon Lover

Dorothy Allison

KATY ALWAYS SAID she wanted to be the Demon Lover, the one we desire even when we know it is not us she wants, but our souls. When she comes back to me now, she comes in that form and I never fail to think that the shadows at her shoulders could be wings.

She comes in when I am not quite asleep and brings me fully awake by laying cold fingers on my warm back. Her pale skin gleams in the moonlight, reflecting every beam like a mirror of smoked glass while her teeth and nails shine phosphorescent.

"Wake up," Katy whispers, and leans over to bite my naked shoulder. "Wake up. Wake up!"

"No," I say, "not you."

But I knew she was coming. I could hear her echoes peeling back off the moments, the way Aunt Raylene always said she could hear a spell coming on. Katy's persistent. Some of my ghosts are so faded: they only come when I reach for them. This one reaches for me.

"Sit up," she says. "I won't bite you." But her teeth are sharp in the pale light, and I sit up warily. The only predictable thing about Katy was her stubborn perversity; she would mostly do whatever she swore solemnly she would not.

"Shit," I whisper, and roll over. She laughs and passes me a joint. The smoke wreathes her like a cloak, heavy and sweet around us. I inhale deeply, grin up at her and say, "My hallucinations get me stoned."

"Lucky you. It costs everyone else money."

She blows smoke out her nose. Katy has a matter-of-fact manner about her tonight, very unlike herself. It's been three years since she O.D.'d, and in that time she's grown more urgent, not less. This strange air of calmness disturbs me. If the dead lose their restlessness, do they finally go away?

Something falls in the other room, wood striking wood. It's probably Molly going to the bathroom a little drunk as usual, knocking things over. Katy slides up on one knee and clutches the edge of the waterbed frame. If she were a cat her hair would be on end. As it is, the hair above her ears seems suddenly fuller. I reach over and take the joint from her hand, moving gently, carefully soothing her with only my unspoken demand to hold her.

"You going to wake me up in the night," I tell her, "you might as well entertain me. Tell me where you got this delicacy. It's mashed pecan, right? Tastes just like that batch we got in Atlanta that time we hitchhiked up from Daytona Beach."

Still in her cat's aspect, Katy looks back at me, her huge eyes cold and ruthless. Her expression makes me want to push into her breast, put my tongue to her throat, and hear her cruel, lovely laugh again. It would be easy, delicious and easy, and not at all the way it had been when she was alive. Alive, she was never easy.

"You ain't got no taste at all. It's Panama City home-grown." She comes back down on the bed, not disturbing the mattress. "You always talking 'bout that mashed pecan, but first time I got you really stoned on it, you got sick. Spent the night in the bathroom being the most pitiful child. I swear."

"That was Tampa, and that killer Jamaican." I draw another deep lungful of the sweet smoke. "In Atlanta, you got sick and threw up on the only clean shirt I had with me."

Katy gives her laugh finally, and predictably, I feel the goosebumps rise on my thighs. She settles herself so that her naked left hip is against my shoulder. Her skin is smooth, cool, wonderful. I put my hand on her thigh, and she leans forward to sniff my cheek and rub her lips on my eyebrows. I cannot touch Katy without remembering making love to her on Danny's couch with a dozen drunk and stoned people around the corner in the living room; the tickle of the feathers she wore laced into the small braids over her ears, and the cold chill of the knife she always pulled out of her boot and pushed under the pillows, the sheathed blade that always seemed to migrate down to the small of my back.

Most of all I remember the talent with which Katy would bite me just hard enough to make me gasp, her bubbling laughter as she whispered, "Don't make no noise. They'll hear." Even now, after all this time, I sometimes make love holding my breath, trying to make no sound, pretending that it is the way it always was back then, with drunk and dangerous strangers around the corner and Katy playing at trying to get me to make a sound they might hear. It was the worst sex and the best, the most dangerous and absolutely the most satisfying. No one else has ever made love to me like that—as if sex were a contest on which your life depended. No one has ever scared me so much, or made me love them so much. And no one else has ever died on me the way she did, with everything between us unsettled and aching.

I slap her thigh brusquely, pushing her back. "You should have had the consideration to puke into a pot. Ruining that shirt that way. You were always careless of me and my stuff."

Katy nods. "A little. Yeah, I was." She settles back on the mattress, cross-legged and still just touching my shoulder. "But I always made it up to you. Remember, I stole you another shirt in Atlanta." Her hand trading the joint is transparent. I can see right through to her smoky breasts, the nipples dark and stiff. "That cotton cowboy shirt with the yellow yoke and the green embroidery. Made you look like a toked-up Loretta Lynn." She gives her short, barking laugh.

"You still got that one?"

"No, I lost it somewhere."

I remember going home for the service one of the local drug counselors organized. People were standing around talking about the shame and the waste, and Katy's mama slapped my hand when I touched her accidentally. "It should have been you," she'd hissed. "Any one of you, it should have been. Not Katy." Her eyes had been flat and dry. She hadn't cried at all, and neither had I. I spent that night in my mama's kitchen, talking long distance to my lover up north about how everybody had looked, the way Katy's last boyfriend had glared at me from beside his parole officer. I'd hugged the phone to my ear, that yellow cowboy shirt between my fists, wringing it until I was shredding the yoke, pulling the snaps off, ripping the seams. I'd torn that shirt apart, talked for hours, but never gotten around to crying. I didn't cry until months later in the Women's Center bathroom. I'd been stone sober, but I was standing up to piss, my knees slightly bent, my jeans down around my ankles, my head turned to the side so I could see myself in the mirror. It was the way Katy had insisted we piss when we went road-tripping.

"You're the dyke," she'd always said. "Keep your health. Learn to piss like a boy and keep your butt dry."

"Piss like a boy," I'd whispered into the mirror, into Katy's painful memory. And just that easy her face was there, her full swollen mouth mocking me, whispering back, "Like a dyke. You the dyke here, girl. I sure ain't."

So then I'd cried, sobbed and cried, and beaten on that mirror with my fists until the women outside came to try and see what was going on. I'd shut up, washed my face and told them nothing. What could I tell them anyway? My ghost lover just came back and made me piss all over my jeans. My ghost lover is haunting me, and the trick is I am glad to see her.

Katy hands me the joint again, moving her small hands delicately. She smiles when she sees where my glance is trained. She flexes her fist, opens the fingers, and wags them in front of my nose. I laugh and take the joint again.

"I loved that shirt. It was the best present you ever got me."

"You forgetting those black gloves with the rhinestones on the back I got in that shop on Peachtree Street. We always got the best stuff in Atlanta. Didn't we?"

"You just about got us busted in Atlanta."

"Oh hell, you were just a nervous nelly. Thought you were the only woman capable of sleight of hand. You just never trusted me, girl."

"You were always so stoned. You did stupid things."

"I did wonderful things. I did amazing things, and stoned only made me better, made me smoother. Loosened me up and made me psychic. I was doing acid when I got you those gloves. That windowpane Blackie sold us."

"Purple haze. You always talk about the windowpane, but we only did it once. You talk about the windowpane 'cause you like to scare people with the notion of you sticking it in your eyes."

"I only did it once with you. I did it lots with Mickey. We put it in our eyes, in our noses. Son of a bitch even shoved it up my ass."

She crushes the joint out on the bedframe. She is smiling and relaxed now, very beautiful even though I am getting angry. Mickey was the one took her to California after I ran off. Mickey was the one who got her back on junk, left her in the motel room where she overdosed. Mickey was the one threatened me at her memorial service, with his parole officer standing right there sweating in the heat. Mickey was the one I'd told to try it.

Come for me asshole, and I'll cut off your balls and push them up your butt. The parole officer had smiled, and my sweat had turned cold on my back. That wasn't like me, wasn't the kind of thing I'd say. It wasn't even the thing I'd been thinking. It was as if Katy had pushed the words out of my mouth. It was exactly the kind of thing Katy would have said.

But Mickey had overdosed himself at Raiford, and I'd never seen any of Katy's boyfriends again. Just Katy, any time she gets restless and wants to come back. I look at her now and my throat closes up. I cannot make casual conversation, cannot talk at all. I want to reach for her but I am too afraid. She is the vampire curse in my life. You have to invite them back, and part of me always wants her, even when most of me doesn't. Right now all of me wants her, flesh and blood, body and soul.

Katy's thick black eyebrows raise and lower, seeing right through me, seeing my grief and my lust. "Ahhh, bitch," she whispers and it sounds like *lover.* She slips one hand under the sheet and strokes her nails along my leg.

I catch my breath. I could cry but don't. Will we be lovers again? Is she real enough this moment to put her filmy body along my too-tight muscles? She wants to; it shows in the unaccustomed softness in her face. I feel tears run down my cheeks.

Now she says it. "Lover."

"Junkie." I hiss it at her, beginning to really cry, making a hoarse ugly sound in the quiet room. "Goddamn you, you goddamned junkie!"

"Ahh well," she drawls, her fingers still stroking my leg. "It's not a lie." She drags herself over, rocking the bed this time, sliding under the sheet. She arranges her body to cup my side, her toes touch my ankle and her head turns so that her mouth is close to my ear.

"Not a lie, no." One hand caresses my stomach; the other hugs my hipbone.

"Goddamn you!" I try to lie still but start shaking.

"Don't be boring," she says. I feel her tongue licking my cheek, wet and almost as rough as a cat's tongue. My whole body goes stiff, and my hands ball up into fists.

"Why do you keep coming back? Why don't you leave me alone? You weren't worth the trouble when you were alive and you sure aren't doing me any good now." I start to fight her, trying to pull away or push her away. But she is smoke only, a cloud on my skin, and I can't escape her.

"Motherfucker...." I give it up to cry and turn my face into the pillow of her hair. It smells so sweet and familiar, marijuana and patchouli.

Katy's shoulders ride up and down. She arches her back and slides her body over so that her belly is on top of mine. I almost scream from the intensity of the sensation. It feels so good. It feels so awful.

"You loved me." She says it right into the hollow of my ear. "You love me still. Even after you left me, you loved me. You couldn't stand me, and you damn sure couldn't save me. But you couldn't stand it without me either. So here I am. Feel me."

She drums her knuckles on my hipbone. Her teeth nip my neck. I gasp and arch up into her. "I'm part of you," she whispers. "Right down in the core of you."

I pull myself back down and lie still, giving it up. "I know." I push my face up. My mouth covers her, tastes her. Her tongue is bitter honey, sliding between my lips, filling my mouth, pushing my own tongue up to the roof of my mouth, expanding until I think I will choke. But I do not fight. I take her in. I want to swallow her, all of her. If she is a ghost, then why not? She could melt into my bones. We could be the same creature.

My hips begin to rock. My fingers curl up and try to grip her waist. A heated sweat rises all over my body. I want to rise up like steam into her, pull up right off my own bones, become something in the air, a scent of marijuana and patchouli, something sweet and nasty and impossibly sad. But I cannot get hold of her. My very movements seem to push her up and away, the cloud of her becoming mist-like, gossamer and fading.

"No!"

Her thumb is in the hollow of my throat. My own pulse roars in my ears. Her laughter is soft, too soft.

"Stop," she says and it comes from very far away. Too far. "You'll make yourself sick."

"I'll take a pill."

"Junkie." She laughs again. Her pleasure in being able to say that to me almost makes me laugh back. "You take too many pills."

That is too much. I go limp again and look up into her black, black eyes. "Oh, mama," I giggle.

"Ooooh, maaamaaaa." Her mouth draws the words out delightfully, rich with lust. She rocks against me, and I can feel her, the flesh hard and cold and powerful.

"I'll make it interesting for both of us," she promises. Her nails rake me lightly. Goosebumps radiate from every burning pinprick. I am not afraid. I burn. I want her so badly. Like a madwoman, I don't care anymore what is real.

"You move," she tells me, "and I'm gone." The cloud of her lifts and it is all I can do to hold myself still until she comes back down.

"You must hold yourself absolutely still. Absolutely."

Her skin burns me where it touches. I stiffen, holding myself for her. Her weight comes down until I shudder with pleasure. Instantly her body lifts, becomes again a cloud. Her phantom laughter is rich and close. I bite my lips and hold myself still again. She comes down again. So cold. So hot. I groan. She lifts, laughs, rises again. It goes on and on.

Do you love me? Do you want me? Do you remember me? Do you hate me? Do you love me? I love you, love you, lover you, come all over you, come up into the dark of you, the pit of you. Pull me down into the pit of you. Memory and touch and taste. You are never alone, never going to be alone. If you cry, I will. If you scream, I will. If you are, I am.

"I love you," she says.

I am drifting. I have come so much my bones have turned to concrete. Their weight immobilizes me. Katy's hot skin presses all over me. It is so dark, so still. It is the pit of the night, and I am drifting off into sleep. I want to wrap my arms around her and pull her down with me, sleep in the luxury of her embrace. But hours of conditioning stop me, and I do not move. I just slide further down into sleep. She says it again.

"I love you."

"You're dead," I mumble.

Her weight increases, presses down on me. I open my eyes.

"Doesn't matter." She has spread out, filled the room. She is enormous, masses of dark all around me. I am afraid. Suddenly I am deeply, deeply afraid, and when she laughs I feel the cold.

"Doesn't matter at all."

Scorpion Girl
Levi Hastings

Orpheus on the 74

Oscar McNary

I sang triple pit bulls to sleep
on my walk to the bus stop.
At six in the Seattle winter
I waited on the north bank.
Mist wove a winding sheet
around cars, houses, bodies.
I threw my coin to the captain.
Bleached sockets guided the craft
across the canal, into the concrete
teeth of the underworld.

Shades on their way to work blinked awake.
My friend's garlic sweat clouded the air.
I had carried him in a pine box.
A kindle shrouded my seat mate,
but in the window glare, a familiar
black beard forested his jaw.
Don't look.
Across the aisle, my friend's laugh lifted off.
I had shoveled earth into his mouth.
His fingers syncopated into my seatback piano.
Don't reach out.
As I climbed into the streetlight,
I turned, called his name,
and watched his features merge with a stranger's.

from "Preternatural Conversations"
CAConrad

Ed Dorn says
faggots should drink directly
from the sewer
i want to dress
special for this
finger wilderness
in his beard
I.V. drip of
sphinx's blood
"what camouflage
will you wear to hide
in the gingerbread
house?" he asks
"none, I want the witch
to find me EAT ME!"
i prefer a song where
i am fed, "Oh Ed,
if you can't handle
me calling you my
sister I don't need
a brother"

Splinter

Ryan Crawford

Scabbed bark under pink palms. Keith balanced himself against a sitka trunk while the tree's needles and boughs chattered in the evening chill. Crows watched with onyx eyes from the lowermost branches.

"Jermaine!" Eddie called again, stumbling his way over roots and ivy in his black chucks. He nearly lost his footing and swore, but Keith rushed a hand out and braced him.

"You need better shoes," Keith said. He tapped the toe of his boots to the sitka. "Won't get far in those." The earth was like iron that day.

Eddie adjusted his thick black glasses and wiped his nose. "I need to find my boyfriend, is what I need." He checked his phone for the hundredth time and held it up to the steel-gray sky as if to give some hopeful satellite a look. Circling around with his phone held high, Eddie brushed the thistles from the cuffs of his jeans. "Still no bars. JERMAAAAAAINE!"

Keith winced at the volume. He really hated city queens. If it wasn't for this kid's scruffy jaw and perky ass, Keith would have made an excuse to end the search early. Sheila would need feeding soon.

The crows above them suddenly took off shrieking. Keith took a breath and observed the woods around them. Something startled those birds, out to his left, where a single young cedar's branches were left swaying. "Sheila?" he murmured. No dog came running.

Eddie squinted into the clouded sunset as the birds flew off, then looked to Keith expectantly. Keith shrugged. "Stay still. It might be a bear." Eddie's eyes widened behind his glasses and he pursed his lips as if to keep from wailing.

Of course there were no bears on this side of the forest. Bear territory was north of Rhododendron, up toward Hood River and the mountain. But Keith wasn't about to say that now that he had some quiet while following Jermaine's tracks. Just beyond the young swaying cedar was a broken fern frond. Keith trudged over and found the expected shoeprint underneath it. Fresh. Another, beneath a disheveled willow.

"He went to the river. Follow me. Keep quiet." Keith smiled to himself with Eddie behind him. "Don't attract the bears."

Soon they heard the rushing water, saw it through the trees. The river was strong with the mountain's melt, whitecapping around water-smoothed boulders. More shoeprints led up to the riverbank. Then the shoeprints turned into footprints. The footprints led up to a Timberland boot, then its nearby mate, muddy and scratched. When Keith asked if it was Jermaine's shoe, Eddie quailed.

More birds screamed and took flight in the rushes next to the river. "Sheila!?" Keith called. Still no dog came running.

"Jermaine?" Eddie tried. No answer.

Keith slowly crept to the edge of the river, where the footprints disappeared behind a growth of reeds. Something was rustling behind the beach grass and breathing heavily. Keith batted the air behind him, motioning for Eddie to get back. Hunched down and edging closer, Keith used one hand to push away the reeds, the other hand clenched in a fist.

No Sheila. No bear, of course.

"Oh god!" Keith sputtered, stumbling in the reeds.

Jermaine yelled incoherently, stammering swears, scrambling to cover himself with his hands. Finally he formed the words, "What the hell are you doing here!?" His headphones were still in his ears, his eyes scanning desperately for what Keith guessed were his nearby clothes. He finally kept still long enough for Keith to recognize the kid. Immediately his gut turned to mud.

"JerMAINE!?" Keith shouted.

Jermaine's eyes became saucers. "Fuck. Uncle Keith, um, just… gimme a minute."

Keith was prepared to ask what his 24-year-old nephew was doing in the forest, in Rhododendron, in November, and why he hadn't told his uncle that he would be in town. But Jermaine was still very naked, clearly aroused, and obviously mortified beyond recovery.

"What were you doing in the woods alone!?" Eddie cried, hands on hips, feet struggling to keep him sturdy on the beach grass. "And this is your *uncle*? The police sent him out here to help me find you and he turns out to be your *uncle*? Why didn't you tell me you had family in the area when I made the reservations? And why are you jacking off by the fucking RIVER, Jermaine!?"

All the while Jermaine yanked his clothes on. He mumbled about needing some peace and quiet to clear his head. Eddie's left eyebrow cocked just above the frame of his glasses.

"So this was your 'headache?' We came here to get peace and quiet *together*."

Jermaine fiddled with his thumb. "I told you I didn't want to come here. Maybe I needed a breather from the 'together' part. And I didn't think we'd run into..." he looked sheepishly then at Keith. "I don't mean... you know what I mean, Uncle Keith. I wasn't planning on seeing you this time. Jesus," he waved a hand at Eddie, "I was gone one hour and you call the—"

"Shut up, you two," Keith said as he retrieved Jermaine's muddy boots. "I'll call the police and let them know we found him."

"With what bars?" Eddie murmured bitterly.

A crack. A gasp. Behind them, about thirty feet into the woods. They spun around to see swaying branches, but nothing else.

"Sheila?" Keith called.

"Don't attract the bears," Eddie whispered.

"*Bears*?" Jermaine's eyes were saucers again.

"SHUT UP!" Keith shouted. "Stay still."

It was the same young cedar they passed on the way here, swaying with low branches. But it was nowhere near the ferns it was next to before. It was below a tall spruce now. Keith shook his head.

"What is it?" Jermaine whispered.

Keith walked closer to the young cedar. He felt its bark. It was unseasonably warm, especially below the canopy of much older trees. "You boys get back to the B&B. I'll meet you there. I need to find my dog."

Jermaine slinked with what Keith could only imagine was boner-shrinking humiliation, his seething boyfriend behind him, and they disappeared into the woods toward the bed-and-breakfast. Keith made sure they were gone before looking for the original spot where he'd seen the young cedar. It was wide open, with the same shoeprint and broken fern. At a closer look, Keith saw lumpy divots in the ground past the fern, on a path toward him. Looking down, he saw he was standing on one. He turned to find more divots trailing behind him. The last one led up to where the young cedar sat rooted now, below the tall spruce.

Sweat beaded on his palms as he approached the cedar. He was sure he was going crazy, and never wanted to have Sheila by his side so badly. Keith began feeling the young cedar again, examined its sparse branches. Under his palm, the trunk seemed to push back against him. He gasped and recoiled his hand. "What are you?" he whispered to himself.

Eyes. In a flash, there were molten amber eyes in the bark. Then a mouth sliced itself into the trunk. In a brittle voice, the mouth rasped, "Don't look at me. Please don't look at me." Keith screamed and fell to the ground. The bottom half of the cedar's trunk split in two, bent like knees, and the two lowermost branches swept forward to cover those amber eyes. "No me mires. Nunca me mires."

Barking. Sheila had heard Keith's scream and wasn't far off.

With a sharp autumn wind and a flurry of cedar needles, the tree ran (*ran?*) in the opposite direction of Sheila's baying and disappeared into the woods. Twisted dead leaves on the hard forest floor rustled under Keith's quaking body. Sheila arrived, and they couldn't have run back to Sibyl's bed-and-breakfast any faster.

"Must have been having a nice walk alone and lost track of time, I expect," Sibyl went on while dressing a bed for Keith. "Happens to us all from time to time." Jermaine suddenly became very interested in his high top shoes while Eddie glared at him from the corner of his eye. "You just have to be careful out there."

"The bears," Eddie agreed fervently.

Sibyl and Keith stretched the sheets over the bed. "Oh honey, don't be silly, there aren't any bears this far down south." Keith cleared his throat. "But other things have happened here."

She told the story that everyone from Rhododendron knew: twenty years ago, three hikers vanished one morning. Searches went on for months, but no one found any evidence of their whereabouts except a tattered shirt in the river. Keith, twenty-one years old and going to Mt. Hood Community College for his forestry degree, was the one to find that filthy plaid shirt. Those hikers had been staying at Sibyl's cottage; she hadn't left town since. Keith wondered if she hoped they would come back one day. They never did.

Jermaine was in the shower now. After Keith called the police from Sibyl's phone to let them know it was a false alarm, Sibyl naturally invited him to stay for dinner, as she always did, but this time he had to accept; Jermaine was here. They finished arranging his bed so he wouldn't have to drive up the hill at night, talked over Sibyl's roasted quail and sweet potatoes and drank wine. Jermaine's ridiculously yellow trucker cap hid some of his embarrassment from the day. "So," Eddie started. "Mister Sloan."

"Keith, please."

"Keith. How long have you been here? In Rhododendron?" Eddie was looking at Keith, but somehow Keith knew the words were meant for Jermaine, who kept his eyes fixed on his plate.

"Born and raised." Always here. Never leaving. Single and lovelorn after a nine year relationship was unhinged by a nineteen year old slut. Rooted. Stuck.

"It seems like a great area," Eddie graced. "It really called to us when we were looking for a getaway for our second anniversary." He took a sip of wine. "Funny how it's such a small town and you've lived here your whole life, but Jermaine never mentioned his family when we booked the reservation."

Sibyl laughed from her seat. Jermaine said nothing.

"I guess that would be a surprise. 'Bout as surprising as my nephew being in a relationship with a man for two years without telling me, or his parents." Keith took his time chewing.

Jermaine bowed lower over his plate. "You won't tell them, will you?"

Eddie dropped his silverware down on his plate with a clatter and marched out of the dining room. He said something inaudible and slammed their bedroom door.

"Why wouldn't you tell them, buddy?" Keith said.

Shuffling feet. "You know how it can be. Same reason I didn't tell you."

Sibyl cackled, her wild brown hair drifting off her shoulders. "Oh honey, please. You and your Uncle Keith have a lot more in common than an affinity for wandering off in the woods, if you get my drift."

Jermaine looked to Keith across the table, puzzled. Keith mocked a scowl at Sibyl, and smiled at his nephew. "Your parents know about me. They took it great. You've got nothing to worry about."

"Oh, no," Jermaine laughed. "Uncle Keith, they know I'm gay. And they told me you are too. I just haven't told them about…"

Keith sucked on his teeth. "Eddie?"

Jermaine nodded. "But for all he knows, I'm not out to them. For all he knows, that's the reason I haven't told them about him. I didn't want to bring him here, either. I mean, I wanted to see you, but… not with a… not with him…"

Sibyl contributed a drunken "Ooh."

Before Keith could ask him what was going on between the two of them (fearing Jermaine was nervous to introduce a white boy to his family), Sheila began barking wildly at the back door.

"You finish dinner, I'll be back. Probably a coyote." He knew it wasn't. He grabbed his jacket and put a hand on Jermaine's shoulder. "We'll talk more when I'm back, bud."

Gritting. The cold earth was carving his face raw. His head pounded, partly from the initial blow that knocked him unconscious, partly from being dragged by his feet deeper into the forest with his skull bouncing off every root in the ground. Something had happened to make Keith certain he would die that night, but the memory was dashed out of his mind with each new bounce and smack on the forest floor.

"Here," came a hard voice. Immediately, Keith's dragger stopped and dropped his feet. "Tie him up." Keith didn't even try to escape. He was sure he had a concussion and could vaguely feel warm blood on his left cheek. As ordered (by whom?), his legs and hands were bound. "Sit him up against that rock. Lay the dog over there. Kill them both before they wake up."

Keith forced himself to open his eyes. It was hard to pick out features in the dark but he could make out leafy silhouettes as he was propped against a jagged boulder.

"What are you… doing in… my woods?" Keith rasped between pained breaths.

The hard voice gave an acrimonious laugh.

Keith slowly bled and struggled for breath against his rock surrounded by what seemed like three figures in the dark, at least two of them digging a large pit. Keith silently prayed that Sheila would wake up wherever they'd put her and run back home to their cabin on the hill. He had never wanted to be home more. But they hadn't killed him yet. What were they waiting for? Did they want to avoid leaving bloody evidence near Sibyl's cottage and kill him out here once the pit was large enough to be a grave? Plan B: buy time.

"Nice place you got out here."

Silence.

"What did you boys do?"

Silence.

"Had to be pretty bad, hiding out from the law, covering yourselves with bark and branches."

The digging stopped.

"Kill him." A rough wooden limb cracked against his raw cheek, scraping his fresh lesions.

"Killing me makes sense. I saw you. But touch my dog and she'll rip your balls off before she goes for your throats."

Another wooden crack to the face, this time harder.

"Is that necessary?" came a low voice, one of the digging men.

The man closest to Keith, the one who'd hit him, walked up to the others and whispered something out of earshot.

"No we don't. Nobody will believe him," said the low voice. "Just let him go."

"He dies," said the hard voice.

"You said yourself we don't need to become monsters just because we became…" the low voice trailed off. "We don't have to be murderers, too."

"We shouldn't, Jack. It's Keith. You know he's a nice guy," said a brittle voice, the one that came from the man dressed as the young cedar—the one with the yellow eyes.

"Nice guy!? God DAMMIT, you idiot! Why did you let him see you!?" The hard voice—Jack—was in the cedar's face now.

When the cedar offered that maybe Keith would agree to keep quiet about this, or maybe the town would think he was crazy, Jack retorted, "That's a whole lotta 'maybe,' pal. I'm not willing to get killed with pitchforks and torches because you couldn't keep still for five minutes while the fucking forest ranger crosses your path for the hundredth time. Just couldn't resist peeping at that kid by the river."

Like a machine, it finally clicked in Keith's throbbing head. Had they been in the woods this whole time? "I found your shirt, Jack Bristol."

All three kidnappers became so eerily still and silent that Keith couldn't distinguish them from actual trees. "Twenty years ago, I found your shirt." Keith was dizzy. This was impossible. "That must mean…" he nodded to the red-eyed one, "you're Simon Leigh."

"Kill him now," Jack ordered. "We'll get the dog next."

Keith looked to the cedar. "You're Teddy Mendez." The yellow eyes in the wood began to shine. Teddy's head seemed to cock in the dark, the branches above (how did he build that?) swaying to one side.

"You… know who I am?" Teddy's brittle voice whimpered.

There was a forceful snapping sound, a rapid rushing of air, and a solid ligneous crack.

"Let me go, Simon! He dies now!" Jack roared.

"You're going to draw attention," Simon's low voice seethed. "You can't kill everyone in this town." Simon wrenched something out of Jack's hands and threw it to the ground next to Keith. It was a fir limb at least five feet long.

"He *knows*! He's seen us!" Jack shouted. "He knows my name!"

Buying time wasn't going to work much longer. He needed a different currency.

"You were all forty. You had the same birthday. That's what the papers said." Keith tried to remember details, squinting into the night. "You were staying at Sibyl's."

Keith went on to describe what he remembered from that year, the profiles, the stories in the news after the disappearance. The reporters somberly told viewers about Teddy Mendez, a sweet bartender in Portland, whose family searched in vain for months in the forest, crying to the cameras that they wanted their son/brother/uncle back. His pictures on the news and in the paper were always stunning, with his warm brown eyes and an earring under black hair frosted blond. Gay people weren't talked about much in the media back then, but the stories diplomatically referred to him as "popular," "adored," "survived by many friends." The articles that year described Simon Leigh's fruitful profession as the Director of Operations for a technology startup, lamenting how his self-made life and promising career were cut short. Keith couldn't remember if Simon's parents were ever interviewed or not, so he left that part out. But he didn't pull punches for Jack.

"They said you had a partner. 'Roommate,' they called it back then. And a daughter." Jack's emerald eyes glistened beneath what Keith was now sure to be oak leaves. "They stayed the longest. My mother brought your little girl books from the library while your partner looked for you." Jack turned away. Keith could hear him growling. "And here you were, the whole time, while she asked everyday if we'd found her daddy yet. So I'll ask you again: what did you three do to make you do this? To hide out in a forest for twenty years dressed up like idiots, with your families going out of their minds looking for you?"

The leaves on Jack's body shivered with what Keith imagined to be the urge to dump him in the half-finished grave and bury him alive. Teddy's amber eyes, twitching, drifted closer toward Keith in the darkness. In their light, and in faint light of the moon, Keith could make out Teddy's mask. There was absolutely no sign of skin beneath. The eye holes were somehow flush with his eyes, and the mouth was flexible enough to move with Teddy's strained expressions. He knelt down with a pop of his knees and rested a rough hand on the mossy soil. The fingers were long, much longer than normal, but could bend even at the furthest knuckles. The soft sprigs of cedar needles seemed to be growing from the bark that was covering Teddy's forearms. A pulse throbbed underneath and the bark tensed, somehow flexible. Like a tendon. Like skin.

Bile rushed to the back of Keith's throat and pinched it shut. "You... those... aren't costumes?"

"No more!" Jack spat, drawing his attention back to Keith.

"Yes," Simon said, kneeling down. The crinkled crust of his face was definitely timber, but it moved with Simon's brow and cheeks.

Teddy scooted over next to Keith. "I was beautiful once. Now my joints are all stiff and I have no teeth." He traced his spindly wooden fingers lightly over Keith's bicep, across his round belly, caressing his neck and chin with twigs. Teddy's head ticked back and forth as if shaking out a memory. Then he started rambling in frantic English peppered with Spanish, describing how one minute they were walking under the moonlight in these woods, smoking strong weed on their fortieth birthdays, and a moment later they were writhing in pain on the ground as their skin hardened and cracked and their extremities gnarled with knots. He described how their teeth fell out, their hair fell out, and they couldn't imagine what evil they had ever done to deserve such a curse. "I used to have the best ass," he moaned, hiding his face.

Keith had planned it out by now. He would keep them talking about their pasts, then tell them he had to take a leak. He'd turn, cut the makeshift ropes from his hands and ankles with the jagged rock behind him, shove Jack into the pit, grab Sheila, and run to the river. He figured they couldn't swim—

whatever they were. He might freeze, but he couldn't stay. He would go back later with state troopers. He would get Jermaine the hell out of here.

But Jack changed everything.

"I'm sorry, Keith. We had to." He trudged over to Keith's legs on his knobby rooted feet and flexed his claws. "Or I thought we did, anyway. You know, we've watched you for twenty years," He scratched through the bindings on Keith's ankles with sharp fingers, "watched you fill out, heard what you talk to your dog about when you think she's the only one listening. We saw you on what I think was your second or third week on the job. Cute black kid, full head of hair back then, driving right past us. I never thought you could find us." Jack moved on to the rope at Keith's wrists now. "My husband, Tom, he doesn't know it but I saw him too, like Teddy saw you. And just like you did to Teddy, he screamed at me. My own husband. Screamed, like I was a monster or something. He ran faster than I'd ever seen him run, like he thought I was going to kill him." Sap seemed to be leaking from Jack's emerald eye. Keith was only sure it was a tear because Jack immediately wiped it off his wooden face.

Keith's hands were free. He lifted them. He could try to break their legs, could club them, could make a run for it. But Keith instead brought his hands to his raw, bloody face. "With your cozy bedside manner, Jack? I can't imagine anyone would be scared of little old you."

Jack blinked. His usually hard voice rang out in a laugh, not bitter like before but powerful, dense, happy.

The feeble morning sun beamed through the dusty window at Sibyl's. Keith was in bed, his face bandaged, his shoulders aching, his lip swollen. The wooden walls softly reverberated with the sounds of the cottage: Sheila snoring safely next to Keith; Sibyl hammering away at something in her workshop (Keith guessed she was fixing her old gas lantern for him—"Fell down a game trail!?"she'd hollered when she'd seen him at the door, after Jack had helped him to the stoop and run off into the dark. "What kind of tore-up ranger are you?"); a tea kettle whistling; Eddie and Jermaine in the next room talking. Their voices were quiet, even Eddie's, but Keith could make out Jermaine's voice forming the words "wrong," "sorry," "Dad," and what Keith thought was "I love you too." The walls resonated with different sounds after that.

It was eight o'clock. Keith packed his knapsack and hiked out into the cloudy morning light toward the sound of the river. The crows were quiet and squirrels whisked away acorns in the branches above him. The conifers overhead seemed to breathe with the November wind. The mountain air smelled familiarly clean, the sound it made through the pines reassuring. He passed markers in the forest that only he knew. There was the pine Keith remembered seeing before Jack had clubbed him last night and dragged him into the woods. There was the red skid strip in the ground from his face. Keith rubbed his bandage as he walked, felt the taught crinkle of the crow's feet blossoming from the corner of his eye. It felt marvelously human.

And there, beyond the river, that's where they agreed to meet him. They hadn't had a hot meal in twenty years—he would start them off with the biscuits in his bag, see if their mysterious new bodies could handle simple carbohydrates. If that worked, and if he trusted them by then, he would invite them to dinner at his cabin on the hill. He would host them, feed them, teach them about what they missed in the world of people. The internet. Cell phones. Wars. He would break the news about Michael and Whitney and Bea, gently of course. Teddy would be a mess. He would swing by the Mt. Hood National Forest office in Hood River and treat the armillaria fungus Jack hadn't seemed to notice growing on his back. These men had been his first assignment, and he wasn't the type to give up.

Keith waved to a maple, a young cedar, and a knotted oak standing still beside each other across the river. As he approached them, he opened his knapsack and held out the package of biscuits. They smelled like a home should.

"Happy birthday. You're sixty today," he said. "Since you've known me for twenty years, we should probably start being friends now."

Teddy's amber eyes flicked open. He shook his head violently, spraying cedar needles in every direction. "No! No! No! No!" Teddy scratched at his own face with long sharp fingers.

Keith dropped the sack and reached out to Teddy. "What's wrong? What's going on?"

Thick cedar hands gripped Keith's wrists, impossibly strong, splintered. "You see me. But I was beautiful once," he said.

Keith looked over his shoulder at Simon and Jack. They were completely still. "Simon, get Teddy under control!" he cried, but there was no answer. Squinting his eyes, Keith could make out deep gouges in the wood below what should have been Simon's arm, and through Jack's throat.

He looked back at Teddy, whose amber eyes twitched erratically up and down Keith's body.

"Teddy, let me go." Keith tried to wrench his hands free but Teddy's grip was too firm. Splinters bored into his skin.

"You know me," Teddy said. "You know what I was. I was beautiful once." Keith felt his mouth being torn to bloody ribbons beneath Teddy's jagged lips. The yellow eyes held his horrified gaze.

A broken maple. A dead oak. No one witnessed Keith Sloan disappear.

The Botanist

Levi Hastings

What's Worst Is You Can't Ask Him to Use Protection

Jeremy Halinen

If you're dead and not a vampire, I'm sorry to say it, but your love life is going to be severely limited. If you don't get off on microorganisms or worms, your only source for postmortem pleasure is the neighborhood necrophiliac. He may not be very attractive or circle socially in the best social circles, but those are the least of your concerns. You'll soon find yourself pregnant—and how will you rest in peace with a fetus ballooning your uterus like helium forced into a used condom under a massacre of stars?

Feeding Desire

Steve Berman

AT THE SCREEN door, Eddie Schafer stared out at his driveway because against the left front wheel of his battered Ford pickup truck sat a man he had been told was dead. Breakfast—just shy of four in the afternoon, Eddie's usual two cups of instant decaf with plenty of sugar, a fried egg white, a slice of dry toast—churned to muck in the acid pit his stomach became at seeing Walt again.

He thought of calling Stu to tell him Walt Deenan was about alive and…well, not looking well. When Eddie had first met Walt over a decade ago at a Beared Weekend in Cape May, the man had towered over the rest. A lineman, muscle and fat in equal measures, so that, when Eddie had dared Walt a dinner wherever he wanted in town if he could lift Eddie six inches off the ground, the man had done so without even grunting. No, he had grinned through wisps of an untamed grizzly beard.

But this Walt, in soiled t-shirt and denim overalls, looked more like an avalanche than a mountain man. His balding head sunk into his chest, that beard gone, replaced by jowls covered in stubble, neck all but lost beneath a thick band of fat whiter than his t-shirt. His bare feet, splayed out huge like clown shoes, were dark, discolored. Perhaps from dirt, perhaps, from diabetes and neuropathy. Eddie had seen plenty of that over the last few years working as a late-shift transporter at the local hospital.

Stu must have heard wrong about Walt. Stu loved to gossip. Especially if he could drink whiskey while sharing dirt. Though Eddie's ulcerated esophagus couldn't take swallowing alcohol or even soda, he joined Stu at the Bike Stop—Stu's favorite, a biker bar in Philly—on his few nights off. After three drinks, Stu's eyes became shiny and he would lean in close to talk to Eddie. Often he'd grip Eddie's beefy arm or nudge his chin playfully. But another glass or two didn't lead to either of their beds. Stu might stumble or collapse but liquor never left him horny. Maybe that was why they were still friends. Eddie knew he could call Stu at any time, but after however long the conversation, when he hung up he was left with a sense of loneliness. The only cure these days was turning to the empty pillow, burying his face deep, and waiting for whatever he took for sleep that night...sometimes melatonin, but on lucky nights it was Xanax.

At a leather bar in Rehoboth Beach last summer Stu had told him Walt had died from a heart attack. Overweight men like Bears rarely lasted long. Either the heart or the pancreas gave out sooner or later. Stu claimed that was why he drank so much, so cirrhosis alone would get him. Eddie worried over esophageal cancer. He was scheduled to have another endoscopic examination next month. He could have bought a new truck with the out-of-pocket expense. Or a new wardrobe, not that he wore much other than scrubs for work and sweats at home. Comfort had replaced all sense of style, which really was another sign not of a mid-life crisis but a mid-life surrender.

At Rehoboth, Stu and Eddie lifted shots of Wild Turkey—hooch, Stu called it—to toast Walt's passing. Eddie had swallowed fast two shots of amber-colored liquid fire—one for losing a fellow Bear, and one for losing the most memorable lay of his life. His throat shook in pain.

Two shots. The words lingered in Eddie's skull, becoming a hymn begging for a gun right then. If he had a loaded one in hand, he'd feel safe exiting his house. Loaded for bear. He almost laughed, and that acrid bubble of insanity rising in his chest scared him almost as much as Walt's presence.

Eddie glanced up at the sky, sure he'd see a turkey vulture circling overhead, waiting for Walt to complete his collapse right there on the tarmac driveway. Just the other day he had driven past a couple of the birds tearing at a roadkill deer by the side of the road. But no, above was only autumn sun, weak and wan despite the bright blue backdrop.

Then Walt turned his head and stared at Eddie. Like a child's toy, he raised one arm with a jerking motion and waved.

Eddie worried that, if he ignored the visitation and returned to bed, Walt would still be there next time he opened the door—God forbid he do at night. He could imagine how the guy's skin would reflect the yellowish light spread by the bulbs over the garage. Like congealed wax. No, the stuff they used to make candles out of before wax. Tallow. Like the fat he poured off from bacon frying into a mug by the sink. Bile traveled up Eddie's esophagus, stung the back of his mouth.

His entire body tense, as if preparing to tackle a guy in the ER waving a box cutter and demanding Oxy, Eddie stepped out on to his porch. "Hey, Walt. Been a long time."

Walt's jaw dropped. Like a ventriloquist's doll gone slack, Eddie thought. Not many teeth were on view. "Eddie, you critter." The voice, the odd term of affection no one else had ever referred to him as, were vintage Walt. Maybe some recording that had been made ten years ago and hidden in the mound sitting in the driveway.

"Why you here?" It seemed the safest question to ask though the one pounding against Eddie's forehead like a migraine was *What the fuck happened to you?*

"I need you, critter." Walt shook all over—Eddie realized that the huge man was attempting to stand up—then stilled. "I owes a debt and needs a ride. You wouldn't turn me down?"

I could call him a cab. Pay some immigrant to haul him upright and drive him off.

As if he'd read Eddie's mind, Walt shook his head. "You didn't say no back then. I remember on the beach, in the sand. Grit everywhere but you didn't complain. You liked it rough. How my beard scratched your chest, your back, the sand scraping your ass."

Eddie feared that the mound of Walt might move a curdled-milk arm to the crotch of his dirty overalls and touch himself there. That would be too much to see, poisoning a good memory.

"Sure. No need to worry—"

"—I ain't worried, I'm just trapped in debtors' prison is all. I want this over."

"I don't have much time before I have to get to work but if it's nearby…"

Walt nodded. "Not too far. Just can't go it alone."

Eddie readied for the stink as he came closer to Walt. A lot of the guys they brought into the ER from the street had more funk than clothing.

Amazing how body odor could be an encyclopedia of rancidness—ancient sweat, piss and crap, worse if there was a gut wound. Nothing smelled worse than a man's insides coming out. Stu always joked that Eddie wasn't a true bear because he was shy about smells—"You have to be willing... no, eager, to shove your face into the other guy's hairy armpit and just snort the funk in like it was a line of Colombian toot-sweet."

But Walt didn't reek. If anything, despite the shabby state of his clothes, the unhealthy look to his features, he possessed an enticing odor. A musk that triggered Eddie's salivary glands. As Eddie braced his lower back and legs against the truck before slipping his arms underneath Walt's own tattooed slabs to lift him, Eddie inhaled deeply, then, embarrassed, stopped as he pushed Walt against the pickup while he opened the passenger door. His mind tried to identify the scent, working over memories. It came to him as he slipped into the driver's seat: a steak, ruby rare, fresh yet seared from its brief time on a grill or under a broiler.

Eddie turned the key in the ignition. He could not imagine how Walt had managed to find his way to his house.

Walt didn't bother with the seatbelt despite the constant *bing-bing* complaint that didn't shut off until Eddie was ready to scream. He sat staring straight ahead. "You need to get on to 295 South."

I could take him to the hospital. "You look sick, Walt."

"I'm well past that."

When Eddie grabbed the gear shift, Walt's wide hand covered his. Eddie hadn't even seen Walt's arm move. The hand felt like a cold sandbag over his. A crescent of dirt underneath a broken thumbnail drew Eddie's eyes.

"You'll take me, critter." Walt didn't turn his head, his face remained slack.

"Of course." He anticipated Walt would start to tighten his hold—that Walt's grasp would be like a vise on his finger bones.

But Walt slid his hand off.

On the highway, Eddie kept to the right lane. He drove well under the speed limit though he wanted nothing more than to press hard on the gas pedal and rush Walt to wherever he was headed and be done with the man. Or better yet, attract a Cherry Hill cop. But the cab of the truck had become thick with his own fear and he worried that doing anything to attract attention—from another driver, from the police, from Walt—would send him into a panic and off the road, crashing into the woods. Nightmare thoughts of being trapped in the cab by bent steel and broken tree limbs while Walt leaned close to kiss him filled Eddie's head.

Walt cleared his throat. "I was a cub once—"

"Weren't we all," Eddie said.

"No. Let me say this without you fuckin' interruptin'." Walt sucked in a deep breath for several seconds, as if trying to inflate dying lungs.

"I ain't old. I'm younger than you. I don't care if you think I'm shittin' you—you'll soon enough understand when we get to the Third Horse.

"I was this cub, all of seventeen years worth of envy at the football players. I looked down at my body—I was all puffy titties and belly like a pregnant sow—and in the locker room the older boys who made up the line loomed. Like gods." A gray tongue licked equally colorless lips. "You have anything to drink in the truck?"

"I could stop—"

"No. No, there's no stopping any of this."

Eddie muttered an apology for having a dry cab.

"I miss sippin' a cold beer, feeling the foam fall over my lips and chin. Best head a man can get is from a beer, my daddy always said. Though after I blew a couple of truckers at the local stop, I doubt they'd agree."

"Where are we going?"

"You scared?"

"I-I didn't say that." But Eddie was.

Walt gave out what might have been a laugh but sounded more like an old dog's bark, more sound than fury. "Critter, some men find a lie easy on the tongue. You ain't one of them."

Eddie drove on.

"Take the next exit. You're smaller than before."

"What?"

"Smaller. Lost weight."

"Yeah." After the dismal results of his first endoscopy, Eddie had to give up three-quarters of his diet. No caffeine. No nuts. Nothing spicy. Nothing fried. Like a religious convert, he went to the extreme, vegan, though his devotion lasted only as long as the follow-up examination. Then he slacked off and hoped that over-the-counter meds would solve the problem. But he must have lost thirty or forty good pounds around his stomach and arms since he'd seen Walt last.

"Shame. Soon you'll be gettin' yourself pampered and waxed. Won't be a Bear anymore."

Eddie snorted. On his salary, the only pampering he could afford was seeing a movie at night at the Loews. Not that he could stomach buttered popcorn any more. He used to practically dump a saltshaker over a large bag, until the upper flakes were frosted and tormented his tongue.

"Turn here." Walt's arm pointed at an overgrown turn-off, not a true exit ramp but more a rough road that Eddie imagined was only used by police when they had to relieve fast a bladder full of caffeinated piss in the woods or sneak a nap.

Eddie expected the road to weave through brush and trees, then stop—not curve about and lead to a gravel parking lot, even a deserted one. Or a restaurant, though the red neon lights of the Third Horse BBQ flickered every so often as if ill. An ill heartbeat came to Eddie's mind.

"This the place," Walt said.

Eddie could have snickered at the kitsch of rain barrels on the wooden porch and brass horseshoes on the twin doors if he wasn't in Walt's lumbering shadow. This was New Jersey, the suburbs. Good BBQ was as much an import as Ethiopian food.

Inside, the recorded mournful voice of Johnny Cash sang about rings of fire.

The hostess behind the upright wooden crate painted with a black hobby horse was middle aged. Her faded name tag—*Amelia*—was askew. She had tried to hide her wrinkles beneath thick pancake makeup and had been sloppy applying her lipstick, a garish red that marred her top teeth and one cheek. "Two gentlemen?" she asked as if someone else might step through the swinging doors at any moment. "Did you have a reservation?"

Eddie was going to remark on how there wasn't a single other car parked on the sepia-gravel lot, but before he could Walt muttered, "They're expecting us."

The hostess smiled and motioned to the next pair of doors. "Seat yourself."

As they walked past her, Eddie saw that she sat on a stool behind the crate. And her body ended at the crotch. No legs whatsoever. He stopped and stared. He'd never seen a survivor of such an amputation. Maybe she was a Thalidomide baby?

She offered him an embarrassed grin before turning her head down to the podium where a placemat with a child's maze was half-finished. She picked up a scarlet crayon, a shade that matched her lipstick—or was her lipstick—and began navigating the simple turns, pointedly avoiding meeting his gaze again.

"So I'll be—"

"Critter, I need you to escort me in there," Walt said. "I can't go in alone. I had to bring them someone."

"You buying?" Eddie meant it as a joke but it fell flat.

The Third Horse's dining room was empty except for one booth at the back, by the kitchen doorway, where three old men sat and looked sad over empty plates.

Eddie smelled the distinctive odors of brown sugar, tomatoes, cumin. But not meat on the grill or the smoker. Still, his mouth watered on instinct.

Cash refused to leave the ring of fire. The CD player or stereo was stuck on repeat.

Walt sat down at the nearest table. The wooden chair creaked beneath his weight. The table top was laminate over a collage of slips of paper. Eddie peered closer. Torn betting slips, losers, from the Garden State Park Racetrack, which had closed years ago. Or burnt down. Eddie couldn't remember which happened first.

When the waitress arrived shirtless and missing one breast, the flesh on her right side a massive, puckered scar, a cruel negative to her D-cup other half, Eddie swore. "What the hell kind of place is this?"

"The end," muttered Walt. "This is the end."

A shaky voice behind Eddie said, "Forgive dear Suse for her reticence. She has no tongue. So perhaps I can enlighten you?" A wrinkled hand deposited in front of him a large steak knife, the very tip tooth-edged and gleaming, the rest wrapped in a checkered cloth napkin.

Eddie looked over his shoulder at the grinning, wrinkled face. One of the old men from the booth. He wore a white dress shirt, open wide at the collar to give room for a massive, liver-spotted wattle that eclipsed his Adam's apple.

"Thank you for bringing Mr. Deenan back to us. I myself hate delaying dinner." The old man chuckled. "Since you've been so kind, Mr. Schafer, might I ask if you're hungry?"

"Uh…hungry?" Watching the geezer's wattle sway like a full IV bag of saline became a distraction.

"Yes. You *do* eat meat, I hope. This is a peculiar restaurant. We only serve the most hungry of folk. I'm not talking about a man who picks at his dinner. We don't deal with *vegetarians*—" Spittle from the old man's mouth launched past crooked tiny teeth and landed on Eddie's forehead. "Such nonsense. A body demands protein. Beans aren't protein. They're like eating little turds. No, meat is what we serve here and is the only thing on the menu. So, I ask again, are you hungry?"

Eddie glanced at Walt, who stared down at the table. The other old men from the booth were approaching them, one with a walker, the other swaying as if drunk.

"Well—"

"Before you answer, I want you to be sure you're hungry. Not peckish, not willing to shove a few forkfuls into your mouth. Look at me, at us, we all possess a singular and severe thyroid problem, Mr. Schafer." He gripped his neck a moment with both hands as if to strangle himself. "It leaves us starving. No matter how much we eat, we're ravenous, the acid in our stomachs burns the meat and fat and bone away before we can wipe our lips of the grease. That is hunger. Knowing as you chew away, knowing that before you even swallow, that bite will not satisfy you. Not the next one. You have to empty your plate, lick it clean of the ruddy juices, and demand a second, a third helping to deal with being so hungry."

"I-I…I'm not like that. I mean…I have a medical…a medical problem, too. I just can't eat anything these days. Will tear up my insides."

He watched as the other old men actually pulled back Walt's chair; they didn't look like they had the strength to lift a napkin, but the chair legs squealed against the floorboards and Walt remained seated, almost limp. The waitress kneaded Walt's shoulder.

"Ahh, nothing worse than a diet. A restriction. A limitation we should overcome. But then, you may still be hungry, starving for something else, Mr. Schafer. We get many patrons who come to the Third Horse who are empty, hollowed by insufferable setbacks, failures, miseries. They are hungry for life, a better life, one that is heaped on to a silver platter and just served to them."

"I don't understand…"

"My colleagues and I are offering you the rarest of menus, Mr. Schafer. Do you want to be wealthy? We can fill your bank account, reveal you have several, even ones offshore, places where they roast pigs on spits. Do you desire a mate? We will bring a man to your door who you will want to kiss and suckle on three square times a day. But why just one? A whole feast of men can be your repast."

"This sounds like a bad horror movie, selling your soul to the Devil and all."

The old man laughed. "I'm a gourmand, not a devil. I have no interest in metaphysics or anything ethereal. One might call us simple." The old man leaned closer. His breath was perfumed like a Thanksgiving Day meal. "We yearn for meat, Mr. Schafer. What you would be selling, like your friend did years ago, is your carcass. In return for feeding your hunger, the yearning that keeps you from sleeping at night…" The old man brought a sleeve up to wipe some spittle from the corner of his mouth. "In return, I later get to butcher you, then serve you as the main course."

"This is crazy." Eddie turned to Walt. "What the fuck, man?"

His old friend stared at the swinging doors of the kitchen. "I want this for you, Critter, you deserve some happiness before the end." He turned to face Eddie. A large hand slid a paper napkin toward him. When he stood up his wooden chair fell back and struck the floor, slats breaking apart like rotted kindling. "We're all meat anyway, at least make the time before we're rendered that way into something beautiful."

The Gourmand's wrist moved, an almost fey gesture, and the gleam of a straight razor caught Eddie's eye. A moment later and the blade was brought down with such force that it severed the tip of Eddie's pinkie and sank into the laminated table top. Blood spilled. Eddie screamed, did not stop as he clutched his hand to his chest and looked toward the door. So distant.

The Gourmand yanked the razor free and wiped the blade pristine with a callused thumb. "One should not be rash when offered so much, Mr. Schafer."

"Oh, God. Oh, God," Eddie moaned as the pain shifted from all-encompassing to localized. He looked down at the gore. He could see bone. He had to get out of there. Head to the hospital. Friends there would fix him. "I-I…need to use the john."

"Of course."

He was ready to shit himself he was so scared. The Gourmand gave him a push at the square of his back toward the men's room. Above that door was a crude outline drawing of a man, prehistoric with a club and an oversized dick, like one of those enormous chalk figures on the hills of Britain.

Once the door swung shut, Eddie raced to the sink and turned on the cold water faucet full blast. The pain of pushing his finger under the frigid spray was enough to make him spit a litany of curses, stomp his feet, then gasp.

He looked at his reflection. He had dead eyes, like those of patients fresh on the gurney after a car crash. He wasn't going to make it—

"Whoah, there!" A deep voice, of a man struggling with his own challenge over the fixed porcelain ring, called out from the cheap pine stall nearest the urinal. "Sounds like you're pissing out a kidney stone or two."

Sheet after sheet of coarse paper towel from the dispenser, soaked in the cold water and pressed to his chopped fingertip, helped to stanch the blood flow but did little to soothe the agony.

His reflection in the speckled mirror showed him wearing surgical scrubs. New words like *distal phalanges* and *vinculum* took over his mind, as if someone had force-fed him years of medical school and residency in a matter of moments, but all the information choked his brain and he had to press his forehead to the pane of glass or else retch out the knowledge. The sense of being someone else, of being a different Eddie, a better one, passed in moments.

"They're m-monsters—"

"Only monsters out there are the ones who eat off their plates. And face it, buddy, there's that green-eyed monster inside each of us."

Eddie applied more pressure, as if he could pull the skin and flesh up and over the wound. He felt sick. Cold water was the only thing preventing him from fainting. He needed to sit down, to think, to find a way out of the Third Horse that didn't involve walking past the Gourmands.

He pushed open the second stall. The wet paper around his hand blotched crimson. He sat on the toilet, thankfully a clean white, the bowl empty of all but water.

"They're not devils," the man in the next stall said. He grunted as if trying to earn a few new hemorrhoids. "Ugh, devils you could trick, 'least in stories. But they aren't interested in souls. Just meat. And we're all basically meat when you think about it."

Eddie hung his head between his knees, like his mother had taught him so many years ago—was it grade school?—whenever he felt nauseated. In his peripheral vision, the stalls on either side did not show any legs, any feet, despite his neighbor's voice.

"You're…?"

"Been hiding away in here for as long as I can remember. They don't like to come into the john. Who wants to eat anything covered in shit or piss? Smell's half your sense of taste anyway. So if I stay here, I figure they can't collect.

"What did you ask for anyway?"

"Nothing."

"Really? Huh. Then why you even here? Unless they started hiring delivery boys." The man's chuckle sounded hollow and hoarse.

Was that what he'd become? Bringing Walt to them? Wasn't being an orderly at the hospital nothing more than a glorified delivery boy. Push a patient here, bring him there? He'd never wanted to be so…menial. So insignificant.

He looked up at some of the graffiti on the stall wall. *Purebred gay mouth eager for delicious dick.* Stu's cell phone number followed the deeply scratched letters. Impossible. But Stu loved referring to himself as purebred, never having touched a tit or pussy except as a baby. With his undamaged hand, Eddie reached out to trace the gouged lettering in the wooden wall, to prove he wasn't seeing things. Underneath his fingertip, the etching squirmed, like living tendons. *Be your concubine, Eddie. Be yours.* Do blind men have tactile hallucinations? Ones that make their dicks grow hard?

If not for the pain, he'd swear everything was a horrible dream. Or madness. But sleep or insanity did not make you stuff a hand into the crevice of your armpit and feel blood soak your shirt.

"Well, if you ain't delivering for them, mind doing a pal a favor?"

"I-I—"

"I can't hurt you. Just, come around. Slowly open the door to my stall. I'm dying of thirst. Fuck, even a handful of water would mean so much."

Eddie struggled to stand. He felt unsteady, unsure. If he didn't step away from the toilet, he might never leave, as trapped as the poor guy next to him. As the door swung shut behind him, he looked for windows, vents, any way to exit without going back through the dining area. But there were none.

He tugged at the handle of the first stall. It resisted at first, as if the hinges were old or the door heavy. He glimpsed an empty toilet seat.

"Don't scream. They like that," the other guy said.

And yet, when the stall door swung all the way open, Eddie did scream.

Hanging from one of the hooks meant for suit jackets or coats was the near-limbless torso of a man, clothes in tatters, skin not much better. Jerky, he had a face that looked as rough and stained as a piece of beef jerky. Except there weren't any eyes. The mouth moved, the tongue passed between slack jaws. The one remaining leg, missing everything below the knee, just twitched.

"Just dip your hand in there—" meaning the bowl "—and bring me a sip."

"No!"

"Not like there's pisswater in it. My dick fell off years ago."

As Eddie stood there the waitress entered the men's room. She carried a plate under one arm and a long carving knife in her other hand. Eddie backed against the wall but she walked past him, even gave him a bit of a smile, before she went over to where the man hung and began slicing off a ribbon of leg meat. Eddie stared at the massive scar on her chest, as if she had borrowed one of the craters of the moon.

"C'mon, I know you're still there. Can hear you breathing," what was left of the man on the stall door said while Suse worked the knife. "Just a sip."

Still cradling his injured hand, Eddie rushed out of the men's room.

"Please, Mr. Schafer, take a seat," said the Gourmand as he pulled a chair back from the nearest table.

Walt was gone.

"You're not even bleeding any more."

He wasn't. The pain was gone. He looked down at his hand, let the makeshift damp bandages fall from his skin. The truncated finger ended in a slightly wrinkled tip, as if left too long in the tub.

"Or should I refer to you as Dr. Schafer? I have always found that to be a noble profession. Second only to butcher. The pleasure of a sharp knife. Nothing fits a hand better—no, not even for men of your tastes."

Eddie collapsed onto the waiting chair.

"The secrets behind all meat are the marinade and aging. Master those elements, well, you can take any poor slab," the Gourmand said and gestured with his straight razor at Eddie, "and fool anyone into thinking it's the richest cut."

The kitchen doors swung open. The air became fragrant with roasted juices.

The other old men crowded behind the lead Gourmand. Their clothes were loose on their frail frames, the collars lost to folds of skin around the neck, the cuffs almost vacant except for bony wrists which held aloft a large stainless-steel tray covered by an equally massive lid.

The Gourmand tied a napkin, heavy cloth, not cheap paper, around Eddie's neck with avuncular care. "There now, Eddie. If we're going to share a meal, I feel I can call you by your first name now."

From beneath the lid came Walt's voice, muffled but strong enough to be heard over Johnny Cash. "I had Stu. Beared Weekend. You were off hiking and we fucked on your sleeping bag. Laughed about how you had a crush on both of us. I remember him lying pressed beneath me—he was still covered in sweat and spunk, and I asked him if we should stay bare-ass naked there for you to come back and join us. Know what he said?"

A Gourmand with sunken cheeks lifted the lid with a flourish. Steam rose and temporarily blinded Eddie.

Like the petals of a massive hothouse flower, slices of glistening meat were arranged. Atop the pile rested Walt's head, the skin broiled and seared, the eyes bulging and browned, the mouth agape, peppercorns arranged on the fat tongue sticking out between charred lips.

Eddie found a long-tined fork in his hand. He swore the cooked lips on the head began to quiver so—afraid of what the answer might be—he skewered Walt's tongue.

A rush of sharp spikes, serrated edges, forks, knives, skewers began to empty the platter as all the other Gourmands took their due.

"Have some sauce, Eddie," said the lead one sitting close by. Spittle from his mouth landed on Eddie's face like tears running down his cheek. "Mind your manners, mind your elbows. Remember, gents, we're not savages!"

Anaphora as Coping Mechanism
Ocean Vuong

Can't sleep
so you put on his grey boots—nothing else—and step out
in the rain. *Even though he's dead* you think, *I still want
to be clean*. If only the rain was gasoline, your tongue
a lit match. If only he dies the second his name
becomes a tooth in your mouth. But he doesn't. He dies
when his heart stops and heat retreats into its bluer shades, blood
pooled where it last bursted, slack like rain in a pothole. He dies
when they wheel him away and the priest ushers you out of the room,
your face darkening behind your hands. He dies as your heart beats
faster, your palms two puddles of rain. He dies each night
you close your eyes and hear his slow exhale. Your hand choking
the dark. Your hand through the bathroom mirror just to see yourself
in multitudes. He dies at the party where everyone laughs
and all you want to do is go into the kitchen and make seven omelets
before burning down the house. All you want is to run into the woods
and beg the wolf to fuck you up. He dies as soon as you wake up
and it's November for months. The coffee like water. The song
on the record stuck on *please*. He dies the morning he kisses you
for two minutes too long, when he says *I love you* followed by
I have something to say and you quickly grab your favorite pink pillow
and smother him as he cries into the soft and darkening fabric.
You hold very still as you look out the window, at the streak
of ochre light smeared on the young birch. And you breathe.
You breathe thinking of summer, the long evenings pressed
into smoke-soaked skin. You hold still until he's very quiet,
until the room fades black and you're both standing
in the crowded train again. You're leaning back
into his chest and he doesn't know your name yet, but he doesn't
move. You're letting go of the pole now. You feel his breaths
on your neck and smile for the first time in weeks. And he just
stands there with his eyes closed, the back of your head nestled
in his sternum. He doesn't know your name yet. The train
rocks you back and forth like a slow dance you watch
from the distance of years. His dimples reflected
in the window reflecting your lips as you mouth the words
thank you. And he never dies.

Epilogue

Vincent Kovar

WHY MONSTERS? **I** was often asked after I announced the theme for this volume. Where did this idea come from? The answers lay in the following book reviews for the recently released volume, *Skin Job*. "Monsters, mutants and mad mayhem punctuate this poetic exploration of death and the deadly." Wrote Jack Halberstam. "Rarely has poetry been put to such ghastly use. The results are horrifyingly great." Another reviewer, David Kirby, added, "Those of you who have long suspected that Evan J. Peterson is the love child of Bette Davis and the Marquis de Sade will find your suspicions confirmed here."

Monsters, I said to myself, that's what I want next, and this Peterson fellow sounds like just the person I want to do it. Fortunately for me and this book, he was lured into the monstrous task of editing this volume.

What is a monster? The word is the modern equivalent of the Latin *monstrum*, which described a dark omen from the gods, usually in the form of something twisted and perverted from the natural order. Even deeper, the word comes from the root *monere*, to warn.

But what do monsters warn us against? Historically they express, not the displeasure of the gods, but the all too-human anxiety stirred up during times of rapid social change. Frankenstein's monster explored the growing primacy of science over religion during the industrial revolution. Jekyll and Hyde cautioned against the new field of Psychology digging around in our heads. Godzilla illustrated just how fragile are the works of man in the atomic age. Sometimes monsters symbolize even more basic emotional excesses: Dracula and sexual desire; the Mummy and forbidden love; the werewolf and the more bestial aspects of human nature.

For generations, LGBT people have been as cautionary monsters in modern morality tales. The pseudo-educational film Boys Beware depicts all gays as sick monsters stalking the beaches and parks to prey on young men. The movie depicts one young man almost falling prey to a pedophile by taking a short-cut home, literally a deviant path, one that is de-via or, off the road.

Holding up LGBT people as omens against angering the gods has a long record in religion as well. Pat Robertson used his platform of the 700 Club to warn that US acceptance of queer sexuality would result in divine vengeance of Greek proportions including hurricanes, earthquakes, and "possibly a meteor." Jerry Falwell claimed that the 9/11 attacks were the result of (among other things) "pagans, abortionists, feminists, gays [and] lesbians..."

But times, they are a changin'. LGBT people are no longer seen as the monsters we once were, but then again, monsters aren't what they once were either.

Chelsea Quinn Yarbro and Anne Rice had thoroughly rehabilitated the vampire, even before Stephanie Meyer turned the creatures into sanguinary disco-balls. The werewolf has never been so attractive. Even the rotting zombie has had a make-over resulting in family friendly monsters and quirky romances such as in the movies Fido and Warm Bodies.

One by one, vampires, werewolves, ghosts and aliens step out of the shadows and onto the road of humanity's mainstream. Every day brings new triumphs. New states open marriage to all. Old laws fall and new ones take their place. While I look forward to the day when all of us stop making monsters of each other, this book is part of my hope that we not entirely lose these fierce creatures of imagination. It has been and always will be the duty of artists to birth monsters. We can't leave it to politicians, doctors and religious demagogues because, as we've seen, they always make a mess of things.

This new world of ours needs fresh monstrum to warn against modern threats and transgressions. What LGBT people may or may not be doing behind the drawn curtains of their bedrooms is of little concern to a population quickly losing all vestiges of privacy. Sex without the biological imperative to reproduce is starting to look benign in the face of an increasingly overpopulated and polluted planet. Even STDs are not so scary when faceless multinationals have re-opened Frankenstein's lab to tinker with our food supply.

So, long live the monster, those delightful little abominations in all of us that dance along the borders of what is permitted and what is not. Though they warn us of what might happen, monsters also open the possibilities to all that could happen: wondrous, delicious, magical possibilities swollen with equal parts horror and delight, impossible and yet absolutely alive.

Contributors

DOROTHY ALLISON makes her home in Northern California with her partner Alix and their son, Wolf Michael. *Bastard Out of Carolina*, her first novel, was a finalist for the 1992 National Book Award. Her second novel, *Cavedweller* (Dutton, 1998), a New York Times Bestseller, won the 1998 Lambda Literary Award for fiction and was a finalist for the Lillian Smith Prize. A chapbook of her performance work: *Two or Three Things I know for Sure*, was published in 1995. *Trash*, first published in 1987, was republished in an expanded edition in 2002. A novel, *She Who*, is forthcoming from Penguin.

ANNE BEAN is a writer of fiction and comics, and is about to graduate with an MFA in writing from Goddard College. When she's not writing books, she designs books. Since fall 2012, she has been the internal layout designer for Minor Arcana Press. In addition, she has designed several chapbooks for Seattle poets as well as the Fall 2012 and Spring 2013 issues of *The Pitkin Review*.

STEVE BERMAN has sold more than a hundred articles, essays, and short stories. He resides in southern New Jersey.

JERICHO BROWN teaches at Emory University. His poems have appeared or are forthcoming in journals and anthologies including, *The American Poetry*

Review, The Best American Poetry, The Nation, The New Yorker, and The New Republic. His first book, *PLEASE*, won the American Book Award, and his second book, *The New Testament*, will be published by Copper Canyon in 2014.

REBECCA BROWN is the author of a dozen books, including *American Romances, The Gifts of the Body* and *The Dogs.* Her work is published in the US, UK and widely translated. A frequent collaborator, she has worked with theater artists, dancers, painters, musicians and the staff of *The Stranger.* Her visual work has appeared at the Frye Art Museum and the Hedreen Gallery and the Simon Fraser Gallery in Vancouver. She lives in Seattle with her wife.

CACONRAD is the son of white trash asphyxiation, whose childhood included selling cut flowers along the highway for his mother and helping her shoplift. He is the author of numerous collections of poetry including *Deviant Propulsion* (Soft Skull Press, 2006); *Advanced Elvis Course* (2009); *The Book of Frank* (Chax Press, 2009), recipient of the Gil Ott Book Award, reprinted by Wave Books in 2010; *The City Real & Imagined* (Factory School, 2010), with the poet Frank Sherlock; and *A Beautiful Marsupial Afternoon* (Wave Books, 2012)

M.S. CORLEY is a freelance illustrator and graphic designer. His interests include but are not limited to Weird Fiction and the early 19th century. He has worked on anything from comic books to video game concept art producing work for clients such as Dark Horse Comics, Simon & Schuster, Microsoft and Amazon Publishing. Corley now lives with wife, daughter and cat named Dinah in Central Oregon. You can view his work at www.mscorley.blogspot.com or on twitter @corleyms

JOHN COULTHART is a British artist and graphic designer whose work has appeared worldwide on vinyl record sleeves, CD and DVD packages, and many book covers. His work as a comic artist includes a collection of HP Lovecraft adaptations and illustrations, 'The Haunter of the Dark and Other Grotesque Visions', which features a collaboration with Alan Moore, and 'Lord Horror: Reverbstorm', a graphic novel with writer David Britton. In 2012 he was voted Best Artist in the World Fantasy Awards.

RYAN CRAWFORD lives in Seattle, Washington, working at a company dedicated to tobacco cessation and weight loss services. His poetry and short stories have been published in *Fragments, Censor This!, Mastadon Dentist, Cerebral Catalyst,* and *Gay City: Volumes 3* and *4.* He believes in marinara, recycling, and the power of acceptance.

CRISPIN FONDLE translates, mistranslates, and mutates poetry and is obviously a nom de plume.

JEREMY HALINEN is cofounder and editor-at-large of Knockout Literary Magazine. His first full-length collection of poems, *What Other Choice,* won the 2010 Exquisite Disarray First Book Poetry Contest. His poems have appeared in such journals as *Cimarron Review, Court Green, Crab Creek Review, the Los Angeles Review, Poet Lore,* and *Sentence.* He resides in Seattle.

LEVI HASTINGS is an illustrator, visual artist and full-time graphic designer in Seattle. From tattooed brawlers to wigged aristocrats, foreign streets to fashion footwear, his illustrations reflect a lifelong obsession with high and low culture, tied together with fine lines and loose watercolor. Raised in the mountains of Idaho, he grew up on a creative diet of dinosaurs, comic books and National Geographic, all of which fed his desire to escape, travel the world and draw everything along the way.

RYAN KEAWEKANE'S short story "Frog in A Well" was published in *Gay City Anthology 4: At Second Glance,* and his first novella Salt was published earlier this year under the pseudonym Kolo. Ryan moved from Hilo, HI, to Seattle in 2003. He quickly fell in love with William Rowden. They have celebrated a decade together. Much of that time was spent traveling the world, learning languages, and diligently obliging the whims of their cat Feistel. Ryan and William recently bought their first house, which is in Shoreline next to a lovely lake.

VINCENT KOVAR is an educational consultant and college instructor living in Seattle. His previous work has appeared in *Icarus, Hardcore Hardboiled* (ed. Todd Robinson), *Touch of the Sea* and *Wilde Stories 2013* (ed. Steve Berman), *A Study in Lavender* (ed. Joseph DeMarco), and *Tales of the New Mexico Mythos: Weird Fiction from the Land of Enchantment* (ed. Paul Bustamonte).

CATHERINE LUNDOFF is the award-winning author of three short story collections: *Crave: Tales of Lust, Love and Longing, Night's Kiss* and *A Day at the Inn, A Night at the Palace and Other Stories*, and one novel, *Silver Moon*. She is the editor of *Haunted Hearths and Sapphic Shades: Lesbian Ghost Stories* and co-editor, with JoSelle Vanderhooft, of *Hellebore and Rue: Tales of Queer Women and Magic*. Her stories have appeared in over 70 publications. Her works and papers are collected in the SFWA/Gender Studies Collections at the Northern Illinois University Library.

JON MACY was part of the early Nineties black and white comics boom with the series Tropo. It was followed by the erotic horror comic series Nefarismo from Eros/Fantagraphics. He is best known for his graphic novel *Teleny and Camille*, an adaptation of the anonymous Victorian novel of gay love attributed to Oscar Wilde and circle, which won a prestigious Lambda Literary Award for gay erotica. His most recent work, *Fearful Hunter*, is the recipient of the 2010 PRISM Comics Queer Press Grant. He lives in the San Francisco Bay Area. www.jonmacy.com

JANIE ELIZABETH MILLER is a poet & essayist whose work explores the environmental imagination. She teaches poetics & environmental literature at the University of Washington Tacoma. Her work has most recently been published in *Written River: A Journal of Eco-Poetics, Tupelo Press* (online), and *Cimarron Review*.

OSCAR MCNARY is a Seattle-based performance poet. He bends syllables into springs and wheels of feral clockwork. He is currently co-editing *In the Biblical Sense: An Anthology of Apocryphal Poetry*.

GREGORY L. NORRIS is a full-time professional writer, published in numerous fiction anthologies and national magazines. He is a former feature writer and columnist at *Sci Fi*, the official magazine of the Sci Fi Channel (before all those Ys invaded). He is the author of the handbook to all-things-Sunnydale, *The Q Guide To Buffy The Vampire Slayer*, the recent *The Fierce And Unforgiving Muse: Twenty-Six Tales From The Terrifying Mind Of Gregory L. Norris* (Evil Jester Press). Norris judged the 2012 Lambda Awards in the Science Fiction/Fantasy/Horror category. Visit him on Facebook and online at www.gregorylnorris.blogspot.com.

EVAN J. PETERSON is a writing professor, freelance editor, and author of *Skin Job* (Minor Arcana Press, 2012) and *The Midnight Channel* (Babel/Salvage Press, forthcoming 2013). His poetry has recently been excerpted in *The New York Times* and his fiction, poetry, and criticism have appeared or are forthcoming in *Weird Tales, The Stranger, Assaracus, Nailed, The Rumpus, Unspeakable Horror 2, Aim for the Head: A Zombie Poetry Anthology,* and *Gay City 4.* He lives in Seattle with a haughty werewolf named Dorian Greyhound. For more, check out evanjpeterson.com.

ANTHONY RELLA is a writer and graduate student living in Seattle. His work has been included in anthologies such as *Mandragora* and *The Full Spectrum.* More about his work can be found at anthonyrella.com.

ARTHUR RIMBAUD was born in Charleville, France in 1854. He wrote all of his (known) poetry between the ages of 16 and 21. Despite his age at the time, he is considered a visionary titan of French poetry. After running away from home to Paris, he became the teenage lover of the poet Paul Verlaine. The two had a turbulent relationship that ended when Verlaine shot him in the hand. Rimbaud died in 1891.

According to **AMY SHEPHERD:** I am a queer writer living in Seattle with my wife Laura and two cats. Raised Baptist in Ohio, I've never quite shed the feeling that I'll someday be struck by lightning for my blasphemous stories. Yet, I can't seem to stop writing them. Visit me at amyshep.com.

IMANI SIMS is a Seattle native who spun her first performance poem at the age of fourteen. Since then, she has developed an infinitely rippling love for poetry in all of its forms. She believes in the healing power of words and the transformational nuance of the human story. Imani is the founder of Split Six Productions (splitsix.com), an interdisciplinary art production company that works towards connecting artists and putting their stories on stage. Her book *Twisted Oak* is available on Requiem Press.

KAT SMALLEY lives in Florida, where she received two BA's in Creative Writing and Philosophy from Florida State University. Her poetry has appeared in issue 5 of *Assaracus.*

JL Smither's poems and short stories have appeared in *Danse Macabre, Tipton Poetry Review, Workers Write: Tales from the Capitol,* and other publications. In addition to a novel, she is also working on a web comic series set in the same universe as "Alexander's Wrath." More information and work is available at jlsmither.com.

Lydia Swartz is an ordinary monster of a sort adolescents do not know how to fear. Her poetry card deck, *Shufflepoems,* will be published by Minor Arcana Press in 2013. Lydia is a flaneur, who (to quote Baudelaire) is "a person who walks the city in order to experience it." Lydia is also a badaud, a gawker who is "absorbed by the outside world, which ravishes her, which moves her to drunkenness and ecstasy." Lydia's motto is solvitur ambulando, which means "It is solved by walking."

Born in Saigon, Vietnam, **Ocean Vuong** is the author of two chapbooks: *NO* (YesYes Books, 2013) and *BURNINGS* (Sibling Rivalry Press, 2010). A Kundiman Fellow, he is a recipient of a 2012 Stanley Kunitz Memorial Prize and an Academy of American Poets Prize. Poems appear in American Poetry Review, Verse Daily, Southern Indiana Review, Guernica, Poetry Northwest and Drunken Boat. Recently, he was awarded a 2013 Poets House Emerging Writers Fellowship. He lives in Brooklyn, NY. (www.oceanvuong.tumblr.com)

ABOUT GAY CITY

Gay City Does.

Gay City Health Project is a multicultural gay men's health organization and the leading provider of HIV and STI testing in King County. Our mission is to **promote wellness in LGBT communities by providing health services, connecting people to resources, fostering arts, and building community.**

Since 1995, Gay City has been regarded nationally and internationally as a leader in messaging and programming that is frank, bold, and reflective of contemporary gay culture. With a recent expansion to a new, larger space, Gay City has increased its commitment to supporting programs that respond to the needs of all LGBT individuals, and to promote the comprehensive wellness – physical, mental, social, sexual, and spiritual – of Seattle's LGBT communities. In addition to an expanded Wellness Center, Gay City's new facility includes the 5,000 volume Michael C. Weidemann LGBT Library, Seattle's LGBT Resource & Referral Center, and the Calamus Auditorium, which features a broad range of arts programming. The new Gay City serves as a resource hub and social destination where Seattle's LGBT community will come together to connect with each other in meaningful ways, to reflect on our changing identities and roles in society, and to foster and develop leadership for the years to come.

To learn more about Gay City Health Project, please visit **gaycity.org**.

PROGRAM HIGHLIGHTS

Who has the most options for free HIV/STI testing for gay, bi, and trans guys in King County?

GAY CITY DOES.

HEALTH: Gay City is the leading provider of free, anonymous HIV/STI screening in King County for both individuals and couples. In addition, we offer such community health services as Hepatitis A & B vaccinations and Rapid Hepatitis C screening. Last year we provided nearly 3,000 HIV tests, reaching a record number of gay, bi, and trans men who have sex with men. We continue to reach historically marginalized, under served, and high-risk populations.

Who connects hundreds of LGBT individuals to much needed resources & referrals every year?

GAY CITY DOES.

RESOURCES: Building a healthy community requires more from us than simply providing testing and vaccination services. Gay City provides our clients with access to resources and a community of peers that better enables them to make healthy choices. We are dedicated to promoting the holistic health of all LGBT individuals in the Seattle area: physical, mental, social, political, and spiritual health. We are committed to the vision of a healthy, united, inclusive, gifted, and powerful LGBT community. To that end, Gay City offers programs and resources that touch the members of our community in a variety of ways, including the 6,000 volume Michael C Weidemann LGBT Library, and the LGBT Resource & Referral Program, which provides phone, email, and drop-in referrals to hundreds of Seattle area LGBT resources.

Who has a large, multipurpose auditorium that can be used by any local organizations or community groups for events and performances?

GAY CITY DOES.

ARTS: Art is the voice of any community. Through Gay City Arts, we collaborate with local LGBT artists and groups to present challenging queer art across a wide range of disciplines. including theater, film, spoken word, literary, and visual arts. In addition, we feature our Calamus Auditorium, which is an organizing center and performance space for Seattle's queer arts community.

Who serves as a resource hub and social destination for the LGBT community in Seattle?

GAY CITY DOES.

COMMUNITY: Gay City offers thoughtful and innovative programming that helps to bring Seattle's LGBT communities together, including the Gay City Volunteer Crew, an all ages group of people interested in pitching in and giving back to their community, and Gay City Sports, our contribution to Seattle's vibrant LGBT sports community. With the opening of our new space, Gay City has grown into a comprehensive LGBT wellness organization and a center for the LGBT community.

HOW YOU CAN HELP

Gay City provides programs and services that encourage LGBT people to care for themselves and their communities. This has only happened because of the generosity of people like you, and can only continue with your support. Nearly half of our budget comes from private sources. As the needs of the LGBT community continue to grow, your support becomes even more vital. Gay City is the only gay community based provider of HIV/STI testing and counseling in King County. We are also the only organization in our region primarily dedicated to nurturing the comprehensive health of gay, bi, and trans men. As state budget cuts continue to grow, your support will become even more vital.

You have the power to make an impact. You have the ability to influence the health and future of the gay community by making a contribution to Gay City Health Project.

You can donate online at **gaycity.org/donate**, or send your tax-deductible contribution to:

Gay City Health Project
517 E Pike Street
Seattle, WA 98122

Coming Soon from Minor Arcana Press

Shuffle Poems: A Deck of Verse, by Lydia Swartz

Drawn to Marvel: Poems from the Comic Books
Edited by Bryan D. Dietrich & Marta Ferguson

Also available from Minor Arcana Press

Skin Job, by Evan J. Peterson
ISBN 978-0-9833966-1-1

Zebra Feathers, by Morris Stegosaurus
ISBN 978-0-9833966-2-8

Minor Arcana Press logo designed and painted by Sergio Coya.

Made in the USA
Charleston, SC
01 July 2013